LIFELINES

LIFELINES

Helen Cannam

This first world edition published in Great Britain 2004 by
SEVERN HOUSE PUBLISHERS LTD of
9–15 High Street, Sutton, Surrey SM1 1DF.
This first world edition published in the USA 2004 by
SEVERN HOUSE PUBLISHERS INC of
595 Madison Avenue, New York, N.Y. 10022.

British Library Cataloguing in Publication Data

Cannam, Helen
    Lifelines
    1.   Women priests - England - Durham - Fiction
    2.   Foot and mouth disease - England - Durham - Fiction
    3.   Country life - England - Durham - Fiction
    I.   Title
    823.9'14 [F]

    ISBN 0-7278-6061-5

Typeset by Palimpsest Book Production Ltd.,
Polmont, Stirlingshire, Scotland.
Printed and bound in Great Britain by
MPG Books Ltd., Bodmin, Cornwall.

For Paul and Barbara, the best of neighbours

One

February 2nd 2001: Candlemas Day. The turn of the year, the moment when winter gives way to spring; the day, Rosalind thought, when I too begin a new season in my life.

The change might not be immediately perceptible in the chill grey day, the dead grasses shivering in the icy wind, but Rosalind felt it all the same, the sense of waiting, of anticipation. Already buds were beginning to form on the bare branches in the hedgerow near where she stood, and there was a new quality in the light, increasing with the lengthening days.

As a child, then a teenager growing up in the country, she had always been moved by the way the seasons of nature were somehow so closely entwined with the pattern of the Church's year, so that they seemed to travel together, step by step. Later, as life took her steadily further away from her country roots, she had lost touch with that sense of a universe, both spiritual and temporal, working in intricate harmony. Today, standing on this cold hill top, it returned to her again with force and she rejoiced in it.

She'd left her parents after lunch to doze beside the sitting-room fire – they had both been tired after yesterday's long journey from their Hampshire home in her brother's car. She had driven out of the village and up a road taken at random until she came to what seemed the highest point on the northerly slope above the village. There she'd parked the car in a convenient lay-by and walked briskly back along the road, unheeding of the wind that buffeted her face, snatched at her hair and her coat. She needed this

1

time to clear her head, to calm her before she took on her new responsibilities. She had gone perhaps half a mile when she rounded a bend to find herself looking over the valley, and the large village spread along the nearer bank of the river that shaped it. Meadhope: solid stone houses gathered about a sturdy mediaeval church, the archetypal country parish – her parish, from this evening, when the Reverend Rosalind Maclaren would be inducted as rector of Meadhope and Ashburn.

She felt both proud that she should have been chosen for this work, and awed, even apprehensive, at the new responsibilities she was about to take on. She could not imagine anywhere more different from her previous parish in Coldwell, with its rows of miners' cottages housing an underemployed population, its grim – and often hopeless – council housing estates. Here the land was green and brown, patterned with dry stone walls which linked farmhouses that looked as if they had grown out of the earth. The village too spread like a natural growth, marred only by a factory or two on its eastern fringe, adjoining a small, tidy, red-brick council estate.

'Don't let anyone kid you – country parishes are a darn sight harder than town ones!' That was what Richard Fryer had said to her when she told him where she was going. Vicar of a run-down parish even more disadvantaged than Coldwell, he was a man who had given his whole life to his calling as few clergy ever did, or could. Of all her former colleagues he was the one she respected most, so she took his warning seriously. 'Believe me,' he'd added, 'I know. I've been there.' She had laughed then and told him she could not imagine him in the country, which was true. She would always think of him surrounded by youngsters most people regarded as beyond redemption, opening his chilly vicarage – he refused to waste his stipend on heating if he could find better uses for it – to anyone who needed a roof over their head, demonstrating God's love in every action every day of his life.

But she knew she was not Richard Fryer and never could

be. What she was about to become was – she hoped and prayed – a good country parson in an honourable tradition that went back through the centuries. 'A Pastor is the deputy of Christ'; so the seventeenth-century poet and priest George Herbert had written, terrifyingly, in his 'Country Parson' which she had read, for purely literary reasons, while at university, returning to it again and again when she began to feel she was called to the same vocation. So great a responsibility, so great a pattern to follow! The cure of souls they called it, her charge to serve every one of the men and women and children gathered in the shelter of these lovely hills.

Rosalind walked a little way down the slope, her eyes never leaving the view before her, her head full of prayers that she might be able to approach the ideal, that she might be enabled, in her way, to demonstrate the power of God's love in action.

Rounding a bend, she found herself passing one of those organically planted farmhouses, a long, low stone building with domestic quarters at one end and byres of some kind at the other, its appearance a little marred by a collection of other outbuildings made of rough stone, odd pieces of wood and some corrugated iron. In the yard, beyond a gatepost marked MIDDLE BYERS FARM, stood a battered Land Rover. A sheepdog barked at her passing but stayed, to her relief, well on the other side of the open gateway. An old stone trough by the back door suggested that in summer the yard might have a more colourful appearance, but now, in early February, it was filled only with a few dry remnants of last year's plants, though the angular green of daffodil leaves was already beginning to pierce them.

Beyond the farm were fields in which sheep grazed – the rough black-faced sheep of this part of the Pennines, their coats grey and tangled. In an enclosed area beside the garden on the sunnier, more exposed side of the house a large sheep grazed alone. It was quite obviously a superior creature, pampered and petted, with its creamy coat and glossy horns. Seeing her, it came to look over the wall,

all eager curiosity. She leaned over and patted it, enjoying the feel of the oily wool beneath her hand – she had never touched a sheep before. The animal bleated and nuzzled at her hand. Rosalind laughed. 'I've nothing for you.'

'She'll be after a treat. Pet lamb, spoiled rotten.' The voice came suddenly behind her and Rosalind jumped. She looked round.

A sturdy man, brown-haired, a little younger than she was – in his mid-forties perhaps – had just emerged from one of the byres carrying a massive bale of hay, which he then hauled across the farmyard to a wall that edged one of the fields where the sheep grazed, or had been grazing until now, when they rushed noisily towards him. She waited until the man had tossed the bale over the wall and turned back again before asking, 'Are they your animals?'

'Aye.'

'What sort of sheep are they?'

'Swaledales. Best kind for this country.'

A little silence, then Rosalind said, 'It's a fine day for the time of year.'

'Could be worse.'

'*Farmers are never satisfied,*' Alastair had warned her. '*The weather's never right, nothing's ever right.*' Well, she could see him smile now, his *What did I tell you?* smile. But she liked the man's open face, and for all his taciturnity he did not seem unfriendly. She guessed he was simply a man with no words to waste.

'Are those your sheep too?' she asked, indicating a flock several fields distant, on the other side of the road. There were perhaps a dozen, their snowy fleeces contrasting starkly with the nearer animals, great solid creatures who looked as if they enjoyed daily baths.

'Why no, they're Oldfields' sheep. Incomers. Townies. Think you can learn farming from books.'

Rosalind thought it wiser not to say that the state of the sheep suggested the townies might have learned something. After all, she herself knew next to nothing about farming. She would have a lot to learn during the coming months about the way of life of these people she had come to serve.

'Nice enough people, mind,' the man added after a moment, a grudging concession to fairness. Then he made his way back to the byre, to bring more hay for his sheep.

Rosalind watched him go. One day soon she would call at Middle Byers Farm as the parish priest, to meet the farmer in her official capacity, and his family too – for there must be a family, judging by the small garments flapping on the line in the garden. For now, she was still in a kind of limbo, resident in the rectory yet without any legitimate role to play, as if she were a ghost, hovering between one life and the next. Technically, until tonight, Meadhope still lacked a rector.

She glanced at her watch; it was time to go home, to allow herself an interval of quiet preparation before this evening's induction service. As she turned to retrace her steps she glimpsed a woman crossing the field beyond the opposite farm, a tall woman with long fair hair tied at the nape of the neck, carrying a bucket towards a hen house around which some strikingly black-feathered hens scratched and strutted. One of the townies, she thought. I'll call on them too. I'll walk up this lovely hill, over these fields, combining duty and pleasure. If I come on my days off then it won't count as dereliction of duty. She had tried not to form too many firm plans for her time here, not until she had got to know the place and its needs. But that was one thing she did intend to do – to visit every household in the parish over the coming weeks and months, until she had visited them all. For most clergy these days such blanket visiting was an unrealizable ideal. But here, as incumbent of these two villages with their small compact populations – about 2000 in total she had been told, when all the outlying farms were taken into account – she could aim to achieve the ideal. To become a part of the community in this place must be so much easier, so much more achievable than it had been in Coldwell, where there would always be people who had no idea who she was. That did of course mean that she would be scrutinized in all she did in a way that had never been the case at Coldwell, but that was something she would learn to live with.

Back at the rectory, she made a pot of tea and took it in to her parents, along with a cake she'd baked. 'I'll have a cup of tea with you now, then I want some quiet time to myself. Alastair's in charge of dinner tonight. Something light, because there'll be refreshments afterwards.' She glanced at the clock. 'He should be back soon.'

'Oh, of course, you said he was going to pick up the children from the station!' said her mother. Living so far from Rosalind, Anne Percival was glad of any opportunity to see her grandchildren, even now they were more or less grown-up. 'Will this be their first visit to Meadhope? I wonder what they'll make of it? Such a pretty place, after Coldwell.'

'It's beautiful. I can still hardly believe I'm here. I feel so privileged.' Rosalind told them a little of her plans and hopes for her new parish.

'Don't expect it all to be easy,' her father warned. 'In my experience country parishes are a good deal harder than town ones.' William Percival was himself an Anglican priest, now retired. 'Not that I ever had more than a very brief experience of an urban parish.'

Rosalind smiled ruefully. 'You're not the first person who's said that to me. I suppose the difficulties in urban areas are obvious enough, so it's easier to be prepared.'

'And people in towns don't expect the vicar to do everything – he's not a traditional part of the community as he is in the country. Also, townsfolk are more ready for change, in my experience. Not so set in their ways.'

'So I can expect more resistance to new ideas? More even than I came across at Coldwell? Oh dear!' She laughed. 'Don't put me off before I've even started! It's a bit late to back out now.'

'Ah, I'm sure you're more than equal to the task,' said her father. He was, she knew, immensely proud of her. He had told her many times that he did not think he could have coped with the strains of life in her previous parish. 'In any case, even in the country things have changed since my day – many more people who work outside the place, for instance, fewer people with their roots in the village. And I know nothing of north country rural life – there are sure to be differences there too.'

'So you wouldn't warn me to turn tail while I still can?'

'Of course not. The one piece of advice I would give – and I'm sure it's one you've taken on board – is to take things slowly, find your feet before you start changing things. But then, that's probably true for every new parish, wherever it is. On the other hand, you always were a bit impatient, a bit ready to rush into things.'

'And if I do that I risk ending up doing everything by myself, taking no one with me. Yes, I know that.' No one, she thought, could ever have accused her gentle, patient yet unassumingly stubborn father of recklessness or impatience. At one time she had thought him exasperatingly set in his ways; now she had come to see that in his steady way he had in fact achieved a great deal. 'I'm going to model myself on you. Then I can't go wrong.'

To her surprise he seemed more alarmed than flattered by the promise. 'Oh no! Don't do that! You're quite a different person. You must find your own way. It's *your* gifts God wants in this place, not mine. Let Him use you and you can't go wrong.'

So that was her prayer when, later, she bent over the kneeling desk in her study and tried to prepare herself for what was to come.

When Linda Emerson came home from work, rather later than she had hoped, there was no one in the kitchen at Middle Byers except Bess, the sheepdog, though the air was filled with a savoury smell – at least someone had remembered to put the casserole in the oven. Bess relinquished her warm place by the range and came ambling over to greet her. Linda fondled the animal's ears with one hand, while reaching out to put the kettle on with the other. She could hear the sound of water running in the scullery. 'Dave!' Her husband emerged, drying his hands on a towel. 'I didn't mean to be so late,' Linda began to explain. 'Anne was off sick. The rest of us had to pick up her calls.'

'Never mind. I put that casserole in the oven like you said. It should be about ready.'

Linda had prepared the meal last night, knowing there wouldn't be much time this evening, though she had not expected to have quite so little. She glanced at the clock. 'Half past five, and we're to be in church by six thirty!' She hung up her coat by the door, slipped off her shoes, began to move around, putting plates and cutlery on the table, making a pot of tea. Dave, hovering in the background, made occasional ineffectual forays into helping her. 'I got lumbered with Ruby Wilson this afternoon – you know, I had care of her last year for a whole month. Never satisfied. Nearly wore me out.' She assumed a quavering whine. '"That's not how I like it. Why can't you do it right? You young people, you don't know how to do anything properly" . . . I suppose I should be grateful for the "young". I don't know how Anne stands it.'

'Maybe that's why she's off sick so often,' Dave suggested. 'Do you have to go tonight?'

'I promised. Though I must admit I could do with stopping in.' Linda, as a former member of the now defunct Meadhope Choral Society, had been invited to help provide a choir for the induction of the new rector.

'But you're not working tomorrow?'

Sometimes, when the agency for which Linda worked part-time was short-staffed, she had to work at weekends. 'No, thank God.' She stood back, frowning, to see if she had missed anything from the table. 'Where are the girls?'

'In front of the t . . . What's that?' A motorbike was roaring into the yard; Dave went at once to the window. Linda, following him, peered over his shoulder as the bike came to a halt, illuminated by the new security light they had installed following a spate of farm burglaries in the area. She gave a squeal of amazement. 'It's Scott!' She ran to open the door.

Her eldest child, creaking in leathers, pulled off his helmet and grinned at the two expectant faces. 'Hi! I'm not too late for supper am I?' He stepped into the kitchen, dropping a bag on the floor and sniffing appreciatively at the savoury-scented air. As he stripped off his leathers, revealing the lanky, dark eighteen-year-old beneath, he laughingly tried to evade his mother's hugs and kisses. 'God, I'm hungry!'

'Never mind being hungry,' Linda put in. 'What are you doing coming back without a word or a call?'

'Oh, so I'm not wanted then! And I thought you'd be glad to see me!' He was grinning as he spoke, utterly confident of his welcome.

'Don't be silly. Of course you're wanted,' said his mother. 'But it's weeks since you've been home. Besides, you always say you don't want to be stuck out here at weekends.'

'Maybe I've changed my mind.' He glanced at his father, who was gazing at him with an expression that mingled bewilderment and delight. 'I'll tell you over supper. Where are the girls?'

The low bass notes of their brother's voice must have reached Vicky and Jade in the next room, penetrating even the chatter of the television. Jade came running in and flung herself at him, full of kisses and exclamations of joy. Vicky followed with fifteen-year-old languor, halting in the doorway to watch. 'What are you doing here?' No stranger, hearing her bored tones, would have guessed she was delighted at the distraction Scott's return had brought to what she saw as her terminally dull life, though Linda could see the tiny marks of pleasure around her mouth and eyes.

Scott, extricating himself, laughing, from his small sister's clasp, acknowledged Vicky with a grin, but said nothing. Linda bent down to open the oven door. 'Right everyone. Supper's ready.'

Once the contents of the casserole had been spooned on to plates, Scott looked round the expectant faces at the table, made sure he had their full attention, and announced through a mouthful, 'I've decided. You know I said I wouldn't be a farmer if you paid me a million? Well, I've changed my mind. I'm coming home for good.'

There was a tiny moment of utter silence, and then everyone spoke at once. He could have had no doubt of their pleasure at his decision. 'I've left Wilkinson's,' he told them. 'Last day today. I'm starting at Armstrongs' in Meadhope on Monday, but only three days a week so I'll be working on the farm the rest of the time. If you'll have me.'

It was not much more than a year since Scott, leaving school with few qualifications, had announced that he couldn't stand farming a moment longer and had found work as a trainee mechanic with a haulage firm in Darlington. Yet here he was claiming to want nothing better than a return to the country life he had spurned! True, he had secured work with a small local haulage firm, whose owner also farmed in a small way, but that would hardly provide him with the urban way of life to which he had so gratefully escaped. Now, only Vicky was prepared to remind him of that. 'Thought you couldn't stand farming. Thought you wanted clubs and nightlife. *People*.'

'I was a kid then. I've had all that.'

Vicky, who if anything craved such an existence even more than her brother had, looked utterly unconvinced. But Scott had already brushed her ambitions aside and turned to his father, who, to his surprise, looked less than happy.

'There's no call to be taking on extra work. You give up that job in Meadhope. If you're coming back to farming, then that's what you'll be doing. There's plenty to keep you busy here, full-time.'

'But I thought . . . well, the way things are, I have to pay my way. I know you can't give me a wage.'

'We'll find a way. If you're going to take over the farm one day – and that's what we're talking about, isn't it, long term? – then you need to put heart and soul into it, all day every day.'

Scott glanced at his mother, who seemed about to speak,

10

but then clearly thought better of it and fell into an uneasy silence. He looked again at his father. 'I've taken the job now. I can't back out.'

'Of course you can. I need you here. It's been tough since you left home, and now with lambing just round the corner . . .'

'Not for a few weeks yet. Tell you what, I'll see how it goes. If we're not managing, I'll hand in my notice. That OK with you?'

'Not really, but don't let's be fighting the moment you're home. We'll talk about it tomorrow. Fancy taking a look at the stock?'

Father and son moved towards the door, the rest of the family clearly forgotten. 'Here, hang on a minute!' called Linda. 'Have you forgotten I'm going out tonight?'

Dave turned back. 'With Scott just home? You're never going now?'

'I don't want to. But I did promise. They need a choir for the new vicar coming. You know that.' She looked anguished, torn. 'It'll only be an hour or two at most.'

'That's OK,' Scott told her. 'I've a lot of catching up to do with Dad. We can talk later.'

Grateful for her son's permission, yet not wanting to leave, Linda watched father and son walk across the yard, while resisting the urge to follow them. Then she gave herself a little shake and hurried upstairs, uneasily, to change.

Two

As Linda drove her battered little Fiat back down the hill her head was full of Scott's unexpected return. She was delighted he was home, of course she was. Dave was right – there was more than enough to keep both of them busy, especially as her work prevented her from helping as much as she would have liked. But she hoped all the same that Dave did not prevail on his son to give up the mechanic's job he had taken on. Scott, like any young man, would want nights out with his mates, new clothes, fuel for his motorbike, as well as basic food and drink. Even as it was, taking her own wage into account, the farm hardly made enough to feed them all, without Scott's hearty young appetite to be satisfied. She wished she could have stayed in tonight, in case Dave proved too persuasive. Dave was a good farmer, with excellent judgement as far as matters of husbandry went; but it was she who did the accounts – Dave hardly interested himself in them at all. He might know, in theory, what the position was, but in practice he put such uncomfortable considerations right out of his mind. She hoped that Scott's obvious good sense would help him to stand firm against his father's arguments.

Knowing the car park beside the church would be full, and probably difficult to get out of at the end of the evening, Linda parked in the main street of the village and set out to walk the two hundred yards or so to the church. At the corner of Church Lane she passed Rose Cottage Guest House. It was finished, then – for weeks before Christmas there had been workmen busy inside and out, modernizing and converting the large old house, neglected for years by the old lady, recently dead, whose lifelong home it had been. Everyone had known it was to be turned into a guest house by some people from Darlington, though no one knew much more than that. Now it was clearly finished, the stonework repointed, paintwork gleaming, an evergreen in a pot either side of the front door, the narrow flower beds that spilled on to the pavement freshly dug, with green shoots already beginning to appear.

At that moment the front door with its shining brass knocker swung open and a woman came down the steps. She looked to be about Linda's age – 44 – a trim, determined-looking woman in a dark trouser suit. Linda smiled at her; the woman fell into step beside her. 'You going to the service too?'

Linda nodded, then gestured towards Rose Cottage. 'Are you a guest or the owner?'

'The owner. Though I've got the new rector's brother staying, with his wife. My first guests.' Her pride was obvious. 'Elaine Robson, by the way.'

Linda introduced herself in turn. 'Have you run a guest house before?'

'No. I've done all sorts but not that. But then my marriage broke up and we had to sell the house. What with a small legacy I had there was just about enough to buy this place. I had a cousin did the work for me, cut price.'

'And now you're running it single-handed?'

'Why yes, I suppose so. But there's not much to do at the moment. And there's Lisa, my daughter – though she's a student and hasn't much time. But she does live at home and she'll help when she can. She'll be on holiday in the busy times.'

'Have you got many bookings so far?'

'A few, round Easter. I've got five rooms, all en suite – three are booked, one just for the holiday weekend. But it's early days. Lisa tells me it's best to start small, until we get into the swing.'

'That sounds sensible.'

The path leading across the churchyard was thick with

arriving guests, a stream that narrowed through the doorway and then spread into the warmth of the church – the heating must have been turned up high all day – and on into the pews, steered this way and that by the sidespeople according to status: county, district and parish councillors towards the front; visitors from the new rector's previous parish at the back; her new parishioners in between; volunteer singers to the choir stalls; clergy of other denominations or from the deanery to the choir vestry, to prepare for the procession that was to begin the service. There was, as yet, no sign of the new rector, whom few had met though she had been resident in the rectory for a few days already, keeping a low profile until she was officially in place.

Linda had never been much of a churchgoer, though she and Dave had been married here twenty years ago, in spite of the fact that Dave's parents had been devoutly Methodist. But this was the place where all her own family rituals had taken place: weddings, funerals, christenings, including those of her children; a beautiful background to most of the important events of her life, looking more beautiful than ever tonight, with candles glowing in every corner, among vases of the spring flowers that were still several weeks from blooming in the dale. Now she took her seat in the choir stalls among the contraltos. 'Good turnout already,' murmured her immediate neighbour, a grandmother called Sheila.

'As she's a woman, everyone wants to take a look at her, I suppose,' Linda suggested. They gazed into the increasing ranks of the congregation, trying to pick out significant figures. 'I see Ted Desmond's there, right in the front.' Ted Desmond was their member of parliament, Labour party to his very backbone, but owing the security of his position more to the larger eastern portion of his constituency – former coal mining country – than to this more rural westerly outpost. Party loyalty being his supreme virtue, he had made a seamless transition from traditional Labour to New Labour and now held a minor government post.

'I'm told that's the new rector's husband,' Sheila told Linda; she was known for being ahead with any gossip that

14

was going. 'There, three rows back, on the end. Scottish. Those must be her children with him.'

The new rector's husband – if it was he – was a slight, fair man, in his early fifties, Linda guessed. He had a faintly pained expression. 'They say he's musical,' her neighbour whispered. In which case, thought Linda, he was probably finding the organ something of a trial; old Mrs Sedgwick was playing some sort of meandering, featureless tune – there had been no adequate organist since the last one had died more than a year ago. As for the two young people beside the rector's husband, one was a gawky lad with 'student' written all over him, the other a beautiful red-haired young woman. She'll break some hearts one day, Linda thought, if she hasn't already. She watched as an elderly couple, one wearing a clerical collar, came to join the family in the pew. 'Her parents, I imagine,' murmured Sheila. 'He's a retired vicar. And –' as a younger couple also caused the seated relatives to stand up and shuffle around '– that'll be her sister and brother-in-law – or was it her brother and sister-in-law? They're staying at Rose Cottage. Did I see you come in with the woman from there?'

There must have been some signal from the back, since before Linda could reply, Mrs Sedgwick suddenly lurched into a new and vigorous – if not entirely accurate – march-like tune. The congregation stood, service sheets at the ready; the choir made sure they had their books open for the first hymn. The young lad carrying the cross at the head of the procession took up his place at the far end of the central aisle before beginning, with stately dignity, to advance. Falling into step behind him were various important church members from Meadhope and Ashburn – mostly people she had known all her life – and more clergy than Linda had ever seen in one place, with the bishop, resplendent in cope and mitre, bringing up the rear. But the person they were all watching was somewhere about the middle of the procession, a slight woman in her early fifties with red hair, an older version of the girl in the family pew: Meadhope's new rector. To the rousing singing of 'Glorious Things of

Thee Are Spoken' the procession moved down the central aisle, eager eyes watching the new rector as she took her place on the end of the front pew in which the visiting clergy were also accommodated.

She had sworn the oaths of allegiance and obedience; she had received the bishop's blessing; she had been led to the door by the archdeacon, to take a symbolic grasp of the handle; she had received the keys of the two churches of Meadhope and Ashburn from the hands of their respective churchwardens. Then she had rung the church bell to signal the moment of taking possession of the cure of souls in this place, conscious that many in the congregation would be counting the number of chimes, since it was said they would indicate how many years she intended to stay in the parish. She had decided to ring it seven times, as a safe sort of number, since she had no idea how long she would be staying. Then, after another small procession, Rosalind was presented with tokens from members of her congregation – a bible, a service book, a priest's stole, a flask of holy water, bread and wine, oil – before being installed in her appointed seat where she was greeted in turn by the other clergy and all possible local dignitaries until her head swam and all the faces seemed to merge into a bewildering mass. Then, to her relief, everything went quiet while the bishop preached, another hymn followed and the final prayers ended with the blessing.

The service was over; Rosalind Maclaren was rector of Meadhope and Ashburn. She disrobed in the vestry, trying to deal warmly with all the congratulations and good wishes around her. Then as she made her way through the church towards the adjoining hall, her father came up to her, enfolding her in a loving embrace. 'Bless you, darling. I'm so proud of you.' She felt tears spring to her eyes, but could think of nothing to say. She knew that did not matter; there was no need to speak.

Refreshments in the church hall were as generous as everyone expected on such an occasion – sandwiches, corned beef pie, sausage rolls, vol au vents, almond tarts, sponge cakes – all the traditional foods – along with a more sophisticated scattering of crostini, filo rolls, and even olives. Rosalind, carried along on a sense of elation and encircling warmth, moved among the throng, trying to speak to everyone. There were old friends from Coldwell, members of her former congregation in astonishing numbers, some clasping her hands with tears in their eyes saying 'I don't know how we'll manage without you!', fellow priests from the team ministry of which she had been a part for the past seven years, since her ordination as a priest. Richard Fryer, her old friend and guide, had come too, as scruffy and lined as ever. The presence of all these people reminded her with a pang of anxiety that here in Meadhope she would be the sole minister of the Church of England – there were others within the deanery of course, but thinly spread over this remote area. In Meadhope itself, her closest colleagues would be the clergy of other denominations: John Parker, a young bearded Methodist minister whom she warmed to at once; the jocular Roman Catholic priest, Father Preston, whose ministry covered most of the dale and beyond; and the Baptist minister, a stocky, pugnacious man for whom, she suspected, ecumenism would have little meaning. She was glad that Alastair was following discreetly behind her as she circulated; he had undertaken to commit the names and occupations of everyone she met to memory, in case she forgot them. She had a good memory for names and faces, but this evening would challenge that ability to the full.

A belligerently hearty voice summoned her attention from just out of her line of vision. 'Daphne Wynyard – Ashburn Hall.' She turned as a woman in her sixties held out a hand for a brisk handshake; she recognized one of those who had played an active part in the service. 'Churchwarden of St John's, Ashburn. Welcome to the country. You'll find it quite a change after a town parish.'

Was there just a hint of scepticism as to Rosalind's ability to meet the needs of the countryside? 'Very different, of course,' she agreed. 'Though human nature's much the same anywhere. But in fact I'm not a complete stranger to country ways. I did grow up in the country, as my father will confirm.' She gestured towards the white-haired figure of William Percival, who was engaged in conversation with the area dean, who was also rector of neighbouring Wearbridge. 'Though admittedly that was in the west country.'

'Ah, hunting country was it?' Daphne's eyes were aglow with an evangelistic fire. 'Do you hunt?'

They had not even been able to afford a horse, even though the vicarage had been equipped with extensive stable buildings; it had been a continuous source of resentment for the pony-mad Rosalind. 'No, though we always used to go and watch the Boxing Day meet.' She remembered the colourful scene, like that featured on many a Christmas card. In those days, she could not remember anyone questioning its appropriateness.

'Then maybe we can interest you in our Countryside Alliance. Big rally in London, March 18th. Of course, hunting's not the only issue. But as a keen huntswoman myself—'

'Is there much hunting round here?'

'We've no hunt based within the dale. Shooting's more of a dale sport. Grouse. But there are a good many of us all the same. Nothing like it . . .' Rosalind wondered if she was already sensing that her companion was a lost cause, for her eyes were wandering. Her gaze fixed suddenly on a point across the room. 'Excuse me, I've just seen Linda Emerson over there. Her son was involved in the fuel protests last year, so I've heard. A likely recruit. No time to lose, I'm afraid.' She shot off through the room. Rosalind smiled ruefully; a one-track mind, clearly. She was relieved she had not been pressed into giving her own views on the Countryside Alliance. She did not think it was her thing at all; but then she had only just returned to country life and knew very little about this place in which she found herself.

Everyone seemed to be jostling for her attention. Next into her line of vision strode a stocky, grey-haired man who introduced himself as Ted Desmond, member of parliament. She tried to ask intelligent questions about the nature of the constituency and its problems, but found that she was soon being harangued at length, in a manner that brought to mind a remark of Queen Victoria's, recalled from a long-ago history lesson. She was said to have complained of her prime minister, William Gladstone: 'He addresses me as if I were a public meeting.' Rosalind stood with what she hoped was an appearance of polite attentiveness, and beyond his shoulder saw that her daughter Sophie was in animated conversation with a fair young woman whom Rosalind knew to be the local vet, beside whom a tweedy young man was trying in vain to gain her attention. Rosalind smiled inwardly. Sophie might have the sort of looks that attracted every male in sight, but she was quite without vanity and immune to flattery – perhaps because she had for so many years hated the knowledge that her looks came from her mother; after all, what girl wants to look like her mother? She was also utterly dedicated to her chosen career; nearing the end of her long veterinary training, she would enjoy talking to someone who was already in the kind of mixed rural practice on which she had set her sights. Her brother Josh, on the other hand, looked rather lost. There seemed to be few people of his own age here, and he was reduced to standing by the buffet table filling and refilling his plate with all the appetite of a student who spent most of his loan on beer.

Then she realized that Ted Desmond had actually asked her a question, and was waiting for a reply. 'Do you know the mining museum at Easthill?' And she had to give him her full attention again while trying to think of an excuse to move on.

When Daphne Wynyard emerged from the crowd beside her, Linda Emerson was standing at one side of the hall with a sausage roll half eaten in one hand and a cooling cup of coffee held awkwardly in the other. Confronted with the tall, formidable figure, Linda instinctively drew back a pace or two. 'Ah, Mrs Emerson! Glad I've seen you. It's your son – forgotten his name, I'm afraid—'

'Scott,' Linda stammered, feeling totally bewildered. What could Scott possibly have to do with Daphne Wynyard? Had this got anything to do with his sudden return home?

'Ah yes, good lad! Took part in the fuel protest last year – that's right, isn't it?'

'I . . . I think so.' Linda seemed to remember that her son had talked about it at the time, during one of their rather unsatisfactory telephone conversations while he was in Darlington. His boss and most of his workmates were enthusiastically involved in disrupting supplies to petrol stations and picketing fuel depots, and he had joined in with all the enjoyment of a youngster made to feel as if he was doing something both important and disorderly. As a worker who needed petrol to do a vital job she had disapproved of what he was doing, so he had never told her very much about it.

'Know how I can get in touch with him? We're trying to get everyone on board for the Countryside Alliance rally in March – London, Sunday March 18th. Think he'd be interested?'

'He doesn't hunt.'

'Doesn't matter. Anyone with the interests of the country-side at heart, that's what we want. Besides, he's worked as a beater for our shoots, odd times. Knows about country ways. How about you – or your husband, come to that? Good farming family. You know the difficulties; you know how little this government understands us. Can we count on your support?'

'Oh, I don't think so,' she said, trying not to sound too dismissive – she did not want to find herself under prolonged fire from this woman's arguments. 'But if you want to speak to Scott he's back home now, for good I think.' She wrote the farm's telephone number on the corner of Daphne's service sheet and then managed, with relief, to find an excuse to push her way to a further corner of the room. Such belligerence made her feel uncomfortable. She was a quiet woman who just wanted to get on with life, undisturbed. Political displays were not her thing at all. She wondered if Scott would be interested, and realized how little she knew about the young man he had become during his months away from home.

When she found what she hoped was a safe place to come to a standstill again, Linda found that she was elbow to elbow with a tall, fair man in an unexceptional suit. She glanced up at him. 'You're the new rector's husband, aren't you?'

He conceded that he was. 'Did I see you in the choir?' he asked. Linda thought she detected a trace of a Scottish accent, then remembered what Sheila had said about him.

'Yes, I'm an alto. Linda Emerson.'

'I was quite impressed,' he said. 'Do you sing for both the main Sunday services?'

'Oh no! We were just roped in for tonight. There isn't a church choir. To be honest, I don't even come to church normally. But we were all in the old Meadhope Choral Society. Our conductor died a year ago – he was the organist here. Since then, we haven't met. I've enjoyed singing again. We all miss it a lot.'

'Can't you find another conductor? One of your own members perhaps?'

'Oh, we've tried. People are either too busy or don't think they're up to it.'

'I'm presently conductor of the Wearside University Choir.'

Linda gazed at him, trying to read his expression. Was he hinting at future possibilities? If so, he should be left in no doubt as to her response. 'You wouldn't like to take us on instead, would you?'

She was aware that Sheila had edged closer to them during their conversation, breaking in, 'Oh, please do! You're just what we need!'

Linda grinned over her shoulder. 'This is Sheila Morris.'

Sheila scarcely paused for breath. 'I went to your choir's concert in Durham cathedral last Christmas. I didn't realize it was you conducting. Of course, we hadn't seen you then. You – they – were wonderful. Do say you'll get us going again!'

'I'll have to think about it,' he said. 'But I don't rule it out.'

'I'll give you my number,' said Sheila. 'Then you can give me a ring if you want me to get the ball rolling. I've got a list of all our old members.' She scrabbled in her handbag, found paper and pen and wrote down a number, which she handed to Alastair. 'I don't suppose you play the organ as well?'

'As it happens, yes,' he admitted, then, laughing, raised a restraining hand. 'But let's wait and see, shall we? I've only just set foot in the village. You can't expect me to barge in and take over. I know quite well that's not going to go down well.'

'We'll do the barging for you,' promised Sheila. 'Won't we, Linda?'

'Of course we will,' Linda agreed; then, with a glance at the clock high on the wall above her head, exclaimed, 'Oh, you'll have to excuse me! I promised I'd not be gone too long! Let me know what happens!'

At last it was over. The dignitaries left and women began to clear away the remains of the food, Josh continuing to help them in the process by eating as if he had no idea where his next meal was coming from, until his sister dragged him away. 'We're going for a drink,' Sophie told their mother, and they left together to compare notes and exchange confidentialities in one of Meadhope's many pubs. Since leaving home they had somehow grown closer to one another than they had been when they were children. Rosalind's relatives had long gone back to their various lodgings; there would be time enough to enjoy their company during the weekend, since they were staying for Rosalind's first Sunday eucharist in her new parish.

Alastair slid a hand under his wife's elbow. 'Home time, I think.'

They walked slowly back towards the rectory, a modern building set in a pretty walled garden next to the church

22

– the former rectory was now the inevitable old people's home. 'A good evening,' Rosalind murmured. She drew a long breath. 'Just smell that fresh air! I'm going to like it here.'

'Me too,' said Alastair. Then he added, with apparent casualness, 'They're desperate for a good organist – well, anyone with an ear for music would know that. What's more, the old one used to conduct the local choral society. When he died it folded for lack of leadership. One or two people told me how keen they were to get it going again.'

'But what about the university choir?'

'I can think of at least two very capable people who'd be keen to take that over. I'll not rush into it, feel my way a bit and see what the possibilities are here. But it could work.'

Rosalind slid her arm through his and nestled close. 'So it could. Then you're glad we came here, in spite of the travelling and everything?' The university, of which Alastair was chief librarian, was on the other side of the county, not far from Coldwell.

'Ask me again in mid-winter, when it snows. But yes, I think so.'

Once at the front door of the rectory, they paused, breathing the clear cold night air, enjoying the near silence. 'I love this place already,' said Rosalind.

Three

It was a Monday, and Rosalind's day off. As she had
determined right from the start, she had spent some of
the day walking one of the local footpaths, taking in visits
to the farms it passed. In the two and a half weeks since
her induction – this was her third day off – she had not
visited as many households as she had originally intended,
for she had already found that, especially at the more remote
farms, she was liable to be seized upon and taken prisoner
with cake and tea and hours of talk by people who rarely
saw anyone outside their immediate family. Once or twice,
where a farmer worked the land alone, she had felt slightly
uneasy, apprehensive for her safety, but no harm had ever
come to her and she acknowledged the loneliness of the life
these people led on their small hill farms.

She had already found that the dale was very different
from the affluent, almost feudal countryside in which she
had grown up, where most of the farms were large and
prosperous, and villages that had once housed poor agricultural workers were now filled with wealthy commuters
and retired people who could afford the high house prices.
There were few wealthy landowners in this place, and it was
lack of work rather than lack of housing that drew the young
from the dale. Until very recently there had been working
lead mines in the dale, the last relics of an ancient industry
that had once meant farming was simply a sideline, but now
the only industries were a handful of quarries, a cement
works some miles to the west, and Meadhope's own small
steelworks.

On this grey, showery afternoon, Rosalind returned by a

24

route she already knew well, across the village playing fields and through the churchyard. She intended, as usual, to slip into church to say evensong and offer prayers for the people she had met today – the Emersons at Middle Byers: Dave, the quietly dedicated man whom she'd met briefly on the day of her induction; Linda, the small brown-haired woman who, she sensed, was the rock on which the household stood; young Scott, who had all the enthusiasm for farming of a recent convert; and the two girls. And, in complete contrast, there had also been Colin Bell, at isolated High Intake Farm.

By now the light was beginning to go, though it was a mild day for mid-February and the sun, briefly appearing, had felt surprisingly warm. There was a particularly sheltered corner of the churchyard where a wooden seat had been planted among a drift of snowdrops. In fine weather there would often be an old man or two sitting on it, enjoying the tranquillity. Today it was occupied by a solitary young woman. She was tall, angular, wearing a waxed jacket and brown trousers, with fair hair pulled back in a pony tail, and she looked to be absorbed in some deeply gloomy thoughts, though she glanced up as Rosalind passed, catching her eye.

'Lovely day,' Rosalind said. The younger woman smiled but made no reply. Rosalind thought she might have seen her somewhere before, but couldn't place her, something that had happened a good deal in these first three weeks in the parish.

Normally she would then have gone on her way, regarding this as a routine casual encounter, but this time some instinct made her pause. She saw the woman was looking at her still, half frowning now. 'Good to see the snowdrops,' Rosalind added, prolonging the moment. 'Have we met somewhere? I'm Rosalind Maclaren, by the way.'

'Sally Oldfield,' the woman introduced herself. 'No, I don't think we've met. You're the new rector, aren't you? We don't go to church. But I've seen you around.'

'You live in the village then? I'm trying to visit everyone in the parish, but it all takes time.'

25

'You'll take a while to get to us. We're up at Moor Farm – we've a smallholding there. Organic,' she added with a livelier note in which pride was evident.

Rosalind placed her then: that first day, carrying a bucket across the distant field. *Townies*, Dave Emerson had said. *Think you can learn farming from books.* She took advantage of the woman's moment of expansiveness to step forward. 'Of course! As it happens, I called there this afternoon, but there was no one in. Do you mind if I join you? My feet! I've walked a long way today.' Sally shifted a little to give her room. 'It must be quite a challenge, going organic.'

'We didn't go organic – it's how we've been right from the start. It just seemed the natural thing to do.'

'What do you specialize in – animals or crops?' Though she knew the answer to that one of course, remembering the pristine sheep.

'Sheep and cattle, in a small way. And chickens. We sell the meat and eggs, mostly by word of mouth. We'll never make our fortune, but we're doing all right. There's a good demand for organic produce, especially with BSE and salmonella and all the other health scares.' Sally smiled faintly. 'I think everyone round here thinks we're a bit mad. But they're very set in their ways – everything has to be done as it always has been done, no matter how the world changes round them. They've all been waiting for us to fail, from day one.'

'And you've proved them wrong.'

'So far.' The enthusiasm that had for a while lit her face faded then, to be replaced by the sombre expression which had first caught Rosalind's attention. 'We can't – couldn't – have children, you see. We thought of IVF, thought of it for a long time. We looked into all the implications and the costs. Money wasn't a problem; we both had good jobs. In the end we decided to accept we just weren't going to have children, that it was the way things were meant to be. We'd sink all our money into this instead, all our energy . . .'

'Wasn't that the right choice?' Rosalind put the question

softly; it was by way of a nudge rather than a probe, something that could be ignored if the other woman wished.

'Yes . . . I don't know . . .' Sally paused, then turned her head suddenly to look Rosalind full in the eyes. 'I've just found out I'm pregnant.'

'Oh.' Had she got the tone right? Was she supposed to offer congratulations? It hardly felt like it. 'Isn't that good?'

Sally forced a shadow of a smile. 'It should be, I know. But – well, the farm takes all our time. We haven't space for anything else. We certainly wouldn't have done it if we'd had children. We don't make enough money, and nothing in farming's really secure. And there are other things – take lambing, for instance. We're only a few weeks away; it's our busiest time, we work without a break, both of us, night and day. Yet it's dangerous for pregnant women to handle sheep – it can cause a miscarriage. How on earth is Ben going to manage without me? And that's just the start . . .' Her distress was breaking through now, her eyes filling with tears.

'Wouldn't it be a good life for children, in many ways?' suggested Rosalind. 'Money isn't everything.'

'I know, but . . .' Sally shook her head. 'It's such a shock . . . I never expected . . .' She blew her nose, trying to keep tears at bay. 'I'm sorry.'

'What does your husband say?'

'I haven't told him yet. I've only just found out.'

'Won't he be pleased?'

'I don't know. He worries enough about little things as it is. I've always been the stronger one, the one who kept things going when they got tough. How on earth is he going to cope with this?' She took a deep breath, like a sigh, then burst out, 'I've even been thinking I shouldn't tell him. Just go and get an abortion. He need never know.' Her glance at Rosalind was almost a glare. 'Now I've shocked you.'

'No you haven't.' Though she had, a little. 'I don't necessarily think abortion is always the worst option. But I'd guess you wouldn't really want to do that.'

'No, probably not.' She sat hunched into herself, as when Rosalind had first seen her. 'It should have been such a happy thing. Why couldn't it have happened years ago, before we took all this on?'

'Sod's law,' said Rosalind.

There was a long silence. Somewhere a blackbird was singing into the gathering dusk. Eventually Sally said, 'Thank you for listening.'

'I wish I could do something to help.'

'You have. Listening is helping. You must have a good face – I don't usually talk about myself like this to complete strangers, especially not about something so personal. But it really has helped. I'm feeling better already.' She stood up, straightening her shoulders, apparently once again the calm and confident woman that Rosalind suspected she was by nature, in full control of her situation. 'Now I'm going to go home and tell Ben. Thanks again.'

Rosalind sent up a prayer as she watched Sally walk away, and then she went into the church, where she added the young woman's predicament to her prayers at evensong. The brief, familiar worship over, she made her way back to the rectory to confront the mundane question of what to cook for the evening meal.

Or so she had expected; in fact, she entered the house to be greeted by savoury smells and the sound of Alastair singing as he cooked – something from Bach's *Christmas Oratorio*, which had been the university choir's last project. She hung up her coat and went into the kitchen. 'I didn't expect you back so soon.'

'There, now I know you never listen to anything I tell you!' The remark was made teasingly; it was an old and amiable wrangle, refuelled when either of them forgot some appointment of the other's which they had been told about in advance. In their busy lives that happened a good deal. 'Tonight's the choir meeting. You know, seven o'clock, church hall.'

She went to kiss him. 'Of course! I remember now. Sorry, love. Hope you get lots of applicants.'

'It's not the quantity I mind about, so much as the quality. Not to mention whether there'll be enough tenors.' He gave the salad dressing he was making a final whisk and poured it over the shredded lettuce already in the bowl. 'Now, let's eat and you can tell me about your day.'

Not wanting Ben to ask too many questions about her absence, Sally had made her doctor's appointment when she knew he would be out, attending his agricultural college course on organic farming remedies. She had simply left a note saying she had gone for a walk, in case she should still be out when he came back. As he had taken the car it was partly true anyway, since, in the absence of a bus service, she would have had to walk to Meadhope and back, a good five-mile round trip.

It was fully dark by the time she pushed open the door into the passage that ran through the house towards the garden beyond. Ben emerged at once from the kitchen to her right, standing over her as she removed her boots. 'Where have you been? I thought something had happened to you!'

'You are a worrier.' She stroked his cheek, already growing stubbly again, though he had shaved early this morning in honour of his trip to civilization. 'How was the course?'

'Useful. What's more, I think I've solved our abattoir problem. Someone gave me the name of one over in Tecsdale.' Until a few months ago, a small abattoir in the dale had slaughtered and prepared their animals for market, but the pressure of increased regulation, and its costs, had forced the place to close. 'I'll go and take a look at it next week. Hopefully we'll have something lined up before the first lot of lambs are due for slaughter.'

'I'm glad. I couldn't bear the thought of sending them miles away to some big place where we've no say in how they do things.' She reached up to kiss him and he put his arms about her.

'I hope you're hungry. I've done one of my lentil stews.'

'Goody!' she responded teasingly. Then, as they entered the kitchen she halted, sliding her arm through his. 'Ben, there's something I have to tell you.' And she did so simply, without embellishment.

His reaction took her completely by surprise. She heard the sharp intake of breath and waited for the dismay to spread over his face. Instead, she saw delight, a pure unalloyed delight, and the next moment he had his arms about her and was lifting her off her feet with whoops of joy. She laughed, struggling to breathe through the fierceness of his clasp. He lowered her gently to the floor and then held her so he could look into her face. 'I love you, Sally – you know that, don't you? This is the best thing that could happen. Now we've got everything.'

Inadvertently she shivered at the presumption of the thought. How could one ever have everything? It seemed like tempting providence even to think such a thing. But his joy was infectious; more to the point, it allowed her for the first time to rejoice herself, to put her fears and doubts aside – or almost put them aside. First, she had to let him know what they had been, what they still were, to some degree. 'But how will we manage? With lambing coming – I won't be able to help. And everything else, all the work. And our profit margins are so low . . .'

'Profit margins!' He tossed the thought aside. 'What do they matter? We've got each other and we'll have our baby. That's riches! As for the lambing, don't worry. I'll manage fine. If it gets tough I'll just think of why I'm doing it. I'll prop my eyes open and remind myself it's not just sheep who give birth.' He kissed her then, a long, lingering kiss. It was some time before they reached the table, or he was able to serve up the stew. Even then they ate little. 'I'm too happy to eat,' Ben said, and Sally realized the same was true for her now. Then her eye caught the clock on the wall beyond his head.

'Don't you want the news headlines?' They nearly always listened to them at this time, a substitute for the newspapers they rarely bought, their one way of keeping in touch with news of the wider world.

Ben reached out to switch on the radio beside him on the

30

kitchen dresser. He grinned and assumed a newsreader's level tones. 'Mrs Sally Oldfield, 37, of Moor Farm, has just found she is pregnant. This . . .' He tailed off into silence, his attention suddenly caught by the words of the actual newsreader. *'A case of foot-and-mouth disease has been confirmed at an Essex abattoir . . .'*

Ben's wry grimace was echoed by Sally. 'Nasty,' he said. 'Hope it stays there.' Then he snapped the radio off and came to take his wife's hands in his. 'Now, beautiful mother-to-be, let's go and shut up the hens and take another look at our baby's inheritance.'

Sally laughed and went with him into the soft evening light.

At Middle Byers, Linda Emerson overheard the news item as she came into the sitting room where her younger children were watching television – or rather, wrangling over their contrary views of a character in the just-finished episode of *Neighbours*. She stood still in the doorway, listening to the end of the brief report, oblivious to the girls' noisy disagreement. Vicky, glancing up as she turned to throw a cushion at her sister, caught the expression on her mother's face and began to pay attention to the television. 'What's foot-and-mouth?' she asked when, at the end of the item, Linda reached for the remote control and plunged the television into silence.

'Oh, a nasty cattle disease. There was a bad outbreak in the sixties.' She smiled reassuringly. 'Long before you were born. Even I wasn't much older than Jade. Now, hurry up and wash your hands. Supper's ready.'

Over the meal, Linda told the rest of the family what she had heard. 'Let's hope they get it under control quickly,' she concluded. 'But I expect they will.'

'It's a long way off,' said Dave. 'Thank goodness.' Essex was far beyond the borders of his mental territory. He banished the thought altogether. 'Well, what did you think of the new lady vicar?' he asked his son. It was the first opportunity they'd had to discuss Rosalind's visit.

31

'OK. She seemed nice enough. At least she didn't ram anything down our throats.'

'A good listener, I'd say,' Linda commented. 'By the way, Dave, who was it phoned just before supper?'

'Oh, that!' A tremor of exasperation passed over his face. 'It was that woman again, the one from Ashburn Hall—'

'Milady Wynyard, Sheila calls her,' laughed Linda.

'Aye, her. Wanting Scott again.' He glanced at his son. 'You were in the bathroom and I couldn't make you hear. She says you haven't given her an answer about the Country-side Alliance rally in London. For heaven's sake hurry up and tell her yes or no and get her off our backs!'

'Will you go?' Linda asked. Scott had said nothing at all to his parents about the matter.

Scott shrugged. 'Doubt it. I'm not interested really.'

'Then tell her!' his father pleaded.

'Rather him than me!' joked Linda.

'I'll tell her in my own good time,' Scott said dismissively.

Vicky, tired of matters in which she was not remotely interested and with concerns of her own, put in, 'I'm stopping over at Rachel's tomorrow night.'

'Please may I stop over at Rachel's?' her mother corrected her, though they both knew Linda was unlikely, in the absence of any good cause, to risk stirring up the inevitable storm that would result if she were to refuse. Vicky had been difficult ever since Scott's return home, which had forced her back to sharing a room with Jade, something she'd thought was well in the past. She resented it furiously and volubly. Her staying away for the night would at least give them all a little peace.

'Isn't this the night for that new choir?' Dave asked his wife.

'It is indeed. I'm looking forward to being able to sing again. I've missed all that.'

'I heard you singing in the bath last night,' Scott said. 'Won't that do?'

Linda aimed a mock swipe at his head. 'You should come along too. They're always desperate for men.'

Scott warbled an octave, teasing, but his mother said, 'There, you've got a fine bass voice.'

'You can count me out. I'm off to the pub tonight.'

'I'll give you a lift if you like. I don't want you riding that bike after a few pints.' It would also give her a chance to be alone with him at last, to try and find out precisely what had triggered his decision to return to farming. It was not that she doubted his commitment to the farm, but she had a strong instinct that there was rather more to it than he had admitted.

'I'll walk if it gets to that. But I wasn't planning on drinking that much.'

That, thought Linda, did not sound as if he was looking forward to the usual gathering with friends in the pub. Was he meeting someone else, someone he wanted to impress? If he was, then this was not going to be the day when she found out. She would simply have to be patient.

A little later, when she went out to the car, she saw Dave securing the padlock on the garage door after putting the Land Rover away. Once, it would have stood out day and night, but the recent spate of farm thefts had made them wary, even though they did not have much in the way of expensive machinery. Dave turned to look at his wife. 'You off then?' He came over to her.

'I'll try and not be late.' She kissed him. 'You must admit, it's working well having Scott home.'

'Aye, well enough. I still don't think he should be doing that job. Take last Friday – I could have done with him to give a hand with tagging the new calves.'

'I know. But you managed, and at least you had him all day today. And the income's a big help. Keeping him fed isn't easy.'

'You can say that again!'

It was, Linda thought, something of a concession. She was sure that before very long Dave would forget he had ever objected to Scott's part-time job. As for her, it simply felt good to have her family all about her again; it was beginning to feel as if Scott had never been away.

33

Four

O n Ash Wednesday, the last day of February, Rosalind
woke to find snow steadily falling. The garden was
already well covered. She thought of this evening's communion service at Ashburn, and hoped the weather would
clear before then. Driving down those narrow twisting roads
would be no fun after freshly fallen snow.

It was not going to be much fun for Alastair either, driving
so far to work. He was already stirring beside her. 'That
wasn't the alarm was it?'

''Fraid so.'

They stumbled round one another, along the landing, into
the bathroom, showering, finding clothes, saying little. Once
downstairs in the kitchen, Alastair peered gloomily out of
the window. 'I had thought I might come to mattins this
morning, but by the looks of it I'd better not risk getting
on the roads any later. With luck I might get through
before the rush. I don't want to get stuck behind some
jackknifed lorry.'

Rosalind kissed him. 'Take care, that's all I ask.'

Before leaving for mattins, she switched on the news,
in case there was anything in particular that required her
prayers. This morning there seemed more than usual: floods,
violence and savagery around the world, new threats of
terrorism in London, a serious train crash near Selby,
with several deaths. And to add to all of that, heard of
just yesterday, a case of foot-and-mouth disease only a
few miles from Meadhope, on a farm in a nearby village.

She put on her thickest winter coat and crossed the
churchyard in the still falling snow, enjoying the childish

sensation of making the first footprints in the unsullied whiteness. Inside the church, the chill enveloped her – there had been no heating since Sunday. She went first to the boiler, in a corner of the choir vestry, to override the time switch. By the time any congregation arrived for the ten thirty communion service the church should be warm. As for herself, she should just about be able to cope with the cold for the length of time it took to say mattins. Afterwards she lingered longer than she might have done as she offered additional prayers for all the farmers in her new parish, facing the terrible threat that had now reached their very doors.

Afterwards – it was still snowing – she made a detour to the newsagents to buy a copy of the local paper. On her way back she saw a van parked beside the road some way ahead, and a man beside it, apparently attaching some sort of notice to the post of a footpath sign. She watched him as he then placed a hood over the sign itself. She'd heard on the news yesterday that local authorities had been given powers to close footpaths; it seemed that their own county council had been quick to make use of them. But then they had every reason to do so, now that the disease had reached here. No more walks on my days off then, she thought ruefully. In any case, she suspected that until the outbreak was under control, no farmer would welcome walkers near his land, still less casual visitors. She could only hope – as she had prayed in church – that it would all be controlled very quickly.

In spite of the snow and news of the disease – or perhaps because of it – there were more people than she expected at the Ash Wednesday communion service; more than last year, as she confirmed when she looked up the figures in the church records, though there was no one from any of the farms, as far as she could tell. Afterwards, a small group lingered at the back of the church, discussing the news. As she came up to them, Rosalind heard one woman say, 'You have to think – all the disasters we've had over the years – BSE, salmonella, now this. There must be something very wrong with our farming methods. All that putting profit before good practice.' She turned to smile at Rosalind, including her in their conversation. Retired headmistress, Rosalind thought, trying to recall her name. 'That has to be true, doesn't it?'

'Up to a point,' Rosalind agreed cautiously. 'But it's not necessarily true of individual farmers, even those whose animals get foot-and-mouth. They say that once the disease is in the country, it takes hold very quickly, and it's highly infectious.'

'And this weather won't help,' Sheila Morris said gloomily. 'Doesn't the cold make it spread more easily?'

Once they had all gone, Rosalind returned the heating to its timed setting and locked the church. At home she had a simple lunch, omitting her usual cup of coffee afterwards – that was to be her practical Lenten offering, agreed with Alastair, who had decided to share it with her. The money they saved would go into the Christian Aid money box that stood on the kitchen dresser.

She had two sick communions to take that afternoon. There should have been a third, to a farmer's wife who was ill with cancer, but her husband had phoned to ask Rosalind not to call – they neither of them wanted to take the risk of infection being brought on to their farm. The other two were in the village itself, and presented no problems. In each case she stayed some time afterwards, to talk to the invalids and their families.

Scott came home from work, covered in oil, stinking of disinfectant. He dashed into the kitchen, peeling off his leathers and leaving them in a heap by the door. 'I see Dad's put a disinfectant mat by the gate.'

'And a bucket too – you have scrubbed your boots, haven't you?' asked Linda, though it was obvious from the smell that he had.

'Course.' He abandoned his outer clothes and dashed upstairs, only to reappear a moment later with a clean but crumpled shirt in his hand, which he held out to Linda, who was at the sink peeling potatoes. 'Darling Mam, best of mothers . . .' Only too familiar with the wheedling 'I love you, Mam' approach that each of her children had perfected in his or her own way, she looked round at him with a wry smile.

'I know, you want me to iron your shirt. If you'd put it away properly when it came out of the airing cupboard it wouldn't need ironing again, would it?'

'I know, Mam, I know.' He smiled his most engaging smile. 'It's all my own fault. But I'm going out again right away, and I do need it. Please!'

Shaking her head fondly, she washed and dried her hands and took the garment, watching him race upstairs again. A moment later she heard the bathroom door open and close, the sound of the shower running, and Scott's intermittent whistle. She smiled to herself as she set to work to iron the creases out of the shirt. This only confirmed her theory about what had tipped the balance in favour of the farm in the boy's mind. Not that she doubted he really had rediscovered an enthusiasm for farming – the energy with which he had involved himself from the moment of his return showed that clearly enough. His work as a mechanic did not seem to hinder him either, though his father was still not quite reconciled to it.

She heard the sound of the bathroom door opening and closing again and glanced at the clock. The girls were watching television as usual, Dave was out with the cows, and now Scott was coming down the stairs at a run, taking several steps at a time. He was transformed, freshly shaved, dressed in his best jeans and tee shirt, his hair carefully arranged. He took the shirt in return for an effusive kiss and slipped it on, unbuttoned, over the tee shirt.

'You smell nice,' said Linda. 'Who is she then?'

'Who's who?' Colour drenched his face, belying the casual tone.

'The girl. The one who made you come home.'

She thought he was about to say he had no idea what she was talking about, in spite of his continuing blush. He opened and shut his mouth, twice. Then he asked, 'How did you know?'

'Mother's instinct. Does she live in Meadhope?'

'Yes.'

'Do I know her?' Born and bred in Meadhope, living in the village until her marriage, Linda knew almost everyone, natives and incomers, apart from those who had only just arrived.

'She's only just moved here. Last month.'

'Ah, so you met her in Darlington?'

The blush had returned in force. He evidently felt the question did not require an answer. 'Mam, don't say anything, will you? I don't want anyone to know – not till . . . well, it's only just . . . you know.'

She patted him on the shoulder. 'I know. Don't worry. Your secret is safe with me. Have a good evening.'

As he moved towards the door, Vicky suddenly came running into the room. When Linda had last seen her she had still been wearing her school uniform – short navy skirt and blue shirt. Now she wore a skimpy lavender top and a brief skirt patterned in pink and mauve. With the make-up she had somehow applied with a speed and energy that would never have been wasted on any task demanded of her by her parents, she now looked at least five years older. 'Scott, wait! I'm coming down to the village with you!'

'I'm going on my bike.'

'I can ride on the back.'

'No you can't. You haven't got a helmet.'

All the eager excitement faded from her face. 'What does that matter? I'm not stopping in when I could be out with my—'

'Just hang on a minute!' put in Linda. 'I can't remember being asked if you could go out. Apart from anything else, none of us should be going backwards and forwards without very good reason. Now, I want to know exactly what you have in mind. And you're not going out without any supper.'

Scott laid his hand on the door latch. 'I'm not hanging around.'

'You can't leave me!' Vicky wailed.

'I'm not going to make myself late for you. Anyway, I told you, you can't come with me.' He pulled open the door just as his father stepped in. 'Just off out, Dad,' he said. 'Don't wait up for me.'

Dave laid a hand on his arm. 'Hold on, Scott!' Scott halted, seething with impatience. 'You're not going anywhere. You're packing in that job, and stopping on the farm. Until further notice.'

'Dad!' The boy was clearly appalled.

'That goes for all of us, for the next two weeks, until we're sure that this new outbreak is just a blip. The less coming and going, the less chance there is of anyone bringing foot-and-mouth on to this farm.'

'Two weeks!' Scott exclaimed. 'But that's not fair! I'm not the only one who goes out to work. What about Mam?'

'That'll go for her too.' He glanced at Vicky. 'And you too, and Jade – no school until we know everything's clear.'

Scott remained where he was by the door. 'I'll bathe in disinfectant night and morning if you want, but I'm not stopping in, not for anyone!'

'You came home to be a farmer. Then behave like one. Put the farm first.'

Father and son glared at one another. Linda braced herself for an almighty row, and was relieved when the telephone rang in the hall. Dave went to answer it and Scott began to argue his case with his mother instead.

Linda felt irritated that Dave hadn't discussed his decision with her before announcing it so baldly, but she saw no reason not to back him up. 'It makes sense, Scott,' she said. 'I know it's hard, but if it keeps the disease off the farm, then it has to be the right thing. I'll be letting them know at work that I'll be off the next fortnight. You do the same – I'm sure they'll understand.'

'More likely they'll give me the push.'

'Then you can look for something else later. It shouldn't be hard, with your skills. Just bear with your dad on this. Please!'

Linda knew it was not the job that would make the self-imposed quarantine such a wrench, but the fact that it would cut him off from this new relationship, almost before it had begun – all the signs indicated a first date, or at least a very early one. She felt deeply sorry for him as he clearly struggled to think of some argument in his favour.

If he was about to find a compelling point to make they would never know, for at that moment Dave came back into the kitchen. His expression was strained, exhausted. He looked straight at Scott. 'I told you not to take that job the moment you came home. I never wanted it. But you knew best, you had to do what you wanted.' Scott was about to stammer some reply to this new and unexpectedly fierce attack of his father's when Dave went on, 'Well, they think they've found foot-and-mouth at Armstrongs'. That was Mike on the phone. You've not to come in tomorrow. Your clothes will want disinfecting, and you – everything. You're not to go anywhere.'

Dave was looking at Scott as if he were a leper; for a moment they all were, somehow seeing in his neat lad-about-town appearance something that threatened them all.

Scott looked round at each of them and then, without a word, gathered up his discarded leathers, opened the back door, dunked the garments into the bucket of disinfectant that stood there and left them in a heap on the yard. Then, still saying nothing, he ran upstairs and shut himself in his room.

Like the Emersons, Sally and Ben Oldfield at Moor Farm also did their best to fence themselves in and shut out the world, as soon as they heard how close the disease had come. There were disinfectant baths at each gateway. They printed their own KEEP OUT notice for the main entrance, where Ben also installed a metal box for their post so the postman had no need to drive up to the house. They made a secure run for their previously free-range chickens and nailed a piece of wood over the cat flap, to stop their cat from wandering. At the end of the day, Ben stood in the doorway and said grimly, 'Well, we've taken all the right precautions.' He gazed at the sheep grazing in the field where they had been pastured for the winter. 'They're going to have to drop their lambs out there, unless the outbreak's over by that time and they let us move them again. Just as well our animals are well cared for, and strong. Let's hope that's enough.'

Over their evening meal he had a further proposal to put to his wife, one that he found hard to put into words. 'Sally, love, I've been thinking. We've agreed we shouldn't be going backwards and forwards, except for very good reasons. I'm giving up my class. We're going to live on what we've got in the cupboards or on the farm . . .'

'Yes, I know.' Sally looked faintly puzzled that he should be stating something so obvious. 'We're lucky to have all those vegetables left in the garden, and a good bit in the freezer. We can still eat well.' She smiled. 'We don't want the baby to want for anything.'

'That's just my point. You need to be able to get to antenatal classes, to the clinic and the doctor's – all that. You know what the doctor said about your age, that he'll want to keep an eye on you. He can't do that if you're stuck up here.'

Sally's eyes widened in alarm. 'What are you saying?' Though she knew the answer before he gave it.

'I think it might be better if you were to go and stay down in the village for a bit. Tomorrow, say – just until this scare's over. You can come home just as soon as we know we're in the clear. Hopefully it won't be long. That way, you get properly looked after *and* we make sure there's the minimum coming and going to the farm.'

'But what about you, all alone up here? No, I can't—'

Ben laid his hand over hers. 'Sally, listen! I'm not saying it's what I'd choose, all things being equal. Of course I don't want you to move out, not even for one single night. But you must see it makes sense!'

In the end, he persuaded her. She telephoned Rose Cottage Guest House, which someone had told her was comfortable and not too expensive, booked herself a room for a few nights and then went to pack her bags.

Alastair was home in good time that evening, having left work early to escape the evening rush. By now the snow had ceased and it had become clear and bitterly cold. 'I'll come with you to Ashburn,' he offered. 'Then at least there'll be two of us if the car gets into difficulties.'

In fact, they reached the hamlet without anything worse than a few uneasy moments – Rosalind's Fiesta had been bought partly with icy surfaces in mind. Daphne Wynyard was already in church, directing little Miss Prentice in the setting out of hymn books. She nodded to Rosalind as she came in. 'If this goes on we'll have all our roads closed,' she said. 'In fact, I had half a mind to ring and cancel today's service.'

Through a momentary twinge of amusement that Daphne should feel it was up to her, without prior consultation, to decide on the cancellation of a service, Rosalind realized suddenly that she was not – as she had immediately assumed – referring to the snow. 'No cases here though?' She had a pang of guilt. Had she increased the likelihood of the disease spreading by driving here tonight from outside the hamlet? Was that indeed what Daphne was implying?

'Not yet. Not looking good. You know there's a case in Meadhope? Not confirmed as such, but it looks pretty certain.'

Rosalind felt cold, with a chill that had nothing to do with the weather. 'I didn't, no.' Dear Lord, help us! she prayed inwardly.

'Armstrongs' haulage. Not many beasts, but they provide transport for most of the farms in the dale. Not good.'

It wasn't good, not good at all. Rosalind knew of Armstrongs' haulage, based in a large yard in a lane that ran close to the council estate, very near to the heart of the village. 'It's such a long way from Essex, where it first started.'

'Yes, well, the days when all farming business was done

at local markets have long gone. Farming's big business now, if not global then certainly national in scale, even continental. One can only hope MAFF's up to the job this time.'

'Do you think they mightn't be?'

'The BSE fiasco was hardly a ringing endorsement, was it? However, BSE had never happened before. They must have learned something about handling FMD from 1967. One would suppose.'

Rosalind recalled all she had heard, at the height of the BSE crisis, about the Ministry of Agriculture, Fisheries and Food being in hock to the farmers. Daphne's tone did not suggest that this was a view she shared. Rosalind might have prolonged the discussion, tried to learn more about Daphne's view at least, but it was nearly time for the service to begin and a trickle of people had already begun to arrive.

It might not have been a large congregation, but as a proportion of the population of Ashburn it was commendably high, Rosalind thought as she tidied away after the service. Outside in the frosty night, the snow lightened the gloom under the trees in the small churchyard. Beyond it, across the road that almost circled it, the jumbled stone walls of the old farmhouses and cottages that formed the hamlet looked chocolate-box pretty beneath their wintry covering, sheltered by the enclosing hills.

'An enchanting place,' said Alastair, who had not been here before.

'I'd invite you to the hall for a cup of tea, but the fewer feet across our threshold the better,' said Daphne as they parted outside the church.

'Will your rally still go ahead?' Rosalind asked.

'Depends what happens in the next week or so. But I'd guess not. Pity. But we'll postpone, not cancel, you can be sure of that. No hunting of course, for the time being. Everything shut down.'

They watched her cross the road to the hall, which was solid rather than graceful, its classical front tacked on to a range of older buildings. Then they drove home, carefully. 'Do you think I should cancel the choir practices?' Alastair asked.

'I should wait a bit and see what happens. After all, most of your members come from within the village, don't they?'

'There's Linda Emerson – and Jack Sheffield, he's a farmer I think. And one or two from Wearbridge, but they'll just be driving along the main road. No, maybe you're right. Give it a day or two at least.'

'Have you settled on Stainer's *Crucifixion*?' Working with a choir he did not know, and who did not know him, Alastair wanted to ensure that they began with a work that was not beyond their abilities, but which all would enjoy.

''Fraid so. We took a vote on it and that's what most of them wanted. Not my favourite, as you know. But it's pretty easy and most of them know it already. We should be able to get it to performance pitch within a few weeks.'

As they turned into the road that led steeply down to the village, they could see a red glow in the distance, to the east. 'Big bonfire,' said Alastair.

'I'm afraid not,' said Rosalind. 'That'll be where they confirmed foot-and-mouth yesterday. It'll be a pyre, to burn the carcasses. There'll be another one before long, I fear, nearer to home.'

'Nasty,' said Alastair. 'Gives a new meaning to Ash Wednesday.'

Five

It was only three days since Dave had placed his family under house arrest, but already they were finding the constant unrelenting proximity to one another difficult to cope with. The house at Middle Byers was spacious, with a large kitchen, a good-sized living room, the once little-used best parlour, now converted to a farm office, and three large bedrooms. But somehow with five people – three of them young and restless – permanently confined there, it seemed to have become more like an overcrowded prison cell. Jade was perhaps the happiest member of the family, whether playing indoors with her toys, or spending time helping her father about the farm, as far as she was able.

Linda tried to keep busy with the domestic tasks for which she usually had too little time, something she would have enjoyed had she not been so unhappy – not so much because she couldn't go to work, though she was very worried about how they were going to manage for money, but because her family was clearly unhappy. Vicky stayed in bed for as long as she dared, leaving as little of the day as possible to be filled before she could ring her friends on her mobile phone to bemoan her fate at length and catch up on the latest gossip. As for Scott, he appeared in the kitchen early on the morning after Dave's decree only to find his father refused to allow him outside the farmhouse. 'I'm not risking you infecting our beasts. You stop in here until we know we're clear.'

Nothing Scott said would change his mind. In fact, apart from these arguments, Dave hardly spoke to his son. He preferred to have Jade's enthusiastic but inexpert help about the farm. Scott took to following Vicky's example and stayed in bed for as much of the day as possible, making long evening calls on his mobile from the privacy of his bedroom. On the Saturday evening, Linda overheard him talking as she passed his bedroom door. Poor love, she thought. All this won't help his cause. Saturday night, and all he can do is talk to her on his mobile.

Downstairs, she stopped Dave just as he was about to go out to give the cattle, still in the byre, their last feed of the day. Jade had already run out ahead of him. 'Dave love, I do understand how you feel, but can't you just relent a bit towards Scott? You know he didn't deliberately put the farm at risk.'

'I can't believe you expect me to let him loose among our animals, in the circumstances!'

'No – no, I don't. But he feels bad enough himself without you rubbing his face in it.'

'Tough!' Then he sighed. 'Ask me again when we know we're in the clear. Until then, I'm sorry, but he'll have to lump it. He should never have got that job. And you should have backed me up when I told him what I thought.'

'He hasn't been anywhere near Armstrongs' animals. He was working in the garage.'

'On cattle transporters. How do you suppose the disease got into the dale in the first place?'

There was no answer to that, so she let Dave go. This, she thought, was going to be the longest fortnight in the history of mankind. Although ten days was, strictly speaking, the incubation period for foot-and-mouth, Dave had insisted on a fortnight, just to be absolutely sure. Linda had looked in her diary that first evening and worked out that it would not be until March 15th that they would be able to breathe freely again and resume some sort of normal life. But since then there had been two other cases of foot-and-mouth discovered within a few miles' radius of Middle Byers, so the longed-for sense of security seemed to be moving ever further into the future.

She set to work preparing supper – pasta and tomato sauce, instant comfort food. Once it was ready, she went to call her two elder children. Scott was still on the phone and made no response. Vicky had come downstairs to see if there was anything she wanted to watch on television, but there wasn't, so she came quickly enough at her mother's summons. She had just slumped down at the table when Jade sneaked in from the yard so quietly that no one noticed her until she was halfway across the room. Linda just had time to register how troubled she looked, to go and put an arm about her, before Dave followed through the door. One look at him was enough.

'Dave . . . ?'

All possible words fled from her. They stared at one another in silence. There was no need for anyone to say anything more, though after a moment Dave said, 'A couple of the cows are sick. Lame, with sores in their mouths. I'm going to call the ministry vet.'

He strode towards the door, which opened as Scott came in. Father and son stood facing one another for a moment. Then Dave glanced round at his wife. 'You tell him. And let him know I'll not be sitting down at the same table as him, ever again. I couldn't stomach it.'

He went out, slamming the door behind him. Scott looked both shocked and bewildered. 'He's gone to phone the ministry vet,' Linda said baldly.

She knew how Scott must feel. Like her, he too would have that dryness in the mouth, the sensation as if he had been kicked in the stomach and all the breath knocked out of him. But worse than that, he must be crushed by the conviction that he had brought this on them.

'I don't want any tea,' he said. His voice was fractured with anguish. Then he too left the room, into the hallway, slipping past his father as unobtrusively as he could to make his way upstairs.

'Will someone tell me what's going on?' demanded Vicky. The tone might be sullen, but she looked frightened.

'Your father thinks two of the cows have foot-and-mouth,' said Linda gently.

'What will happen?'

'If the vet confirms it, then all the animals have to go.'

Vicky glanced wildly at the sheepdog, who had come in at her father's heels. 'Bess too?'

'No, not Bess. She hasn't got cloven hoofs. But all the rest. Every one.'

Jade gave an anguished cry. 'Not Polly!' The pet lamb had always been Jade's favourite.

Linda knelt down beside her and held her close. 'Let's hope it's a false alarm. If not, we're all going to have to be very brave, and help each other all we can.'

Jade pushed her mother away and ran from the room, sobbing her way up the stairs. Linda followed her. When Dave returned to the room, he and Vicky sat down to supper, but neither of them said anything, nor did they eat very much. The pasta lay in thick, unappetizing coils, the sauce chilled; much later, Linda threw it away. She wondered if any of them would ever feel hungry again.

Every incident in that long evening scoured itself into the minds of the family at Middle Byers. The ministry vet came within the hour, agreeing that all the signs indicated foot-and-mouth. Then he said that, though samples would be sent to the laboratory for confirmation, he was not prepared to wait for the results. The disease was already spreading too fast. All the stock must be killed the following morning and then buried in a safe place on the farm – if there was nowhere suitable, the carcasses would be burned. By the time he left, the notices were already up at the gate, printed with words that seemed written in fire: NO ADMITTANCE: FOOT-AND-MOUTH DISEASE.

Scott did not emerge from his room that evening. Linda took a plate of food up to him but he refused it. She wondered if he, like Jade, had been crying. 'Your father doesn't mean what he said. He's just very upset. He'll come round.'

'He's right. I brought foot-and-mouth on to the farm.'

'You don't know that. There are other cases around – as far as I know they haven't had any contact with Armstrongs'. Some people think it comes on the wind.'

'It's more likely it came on my boots, isn't it? Dad needn't worry. I'll keep out of his way.'

Gently, as if he were a small boy again, Linda brushed the strands of hair from his forehead. 'Have something to eat, my pet. You need to keep your strength up. There'll be a lot of work to do to get the farm cleaned up before we can restock – and even more work when we do.'

He stared at her as if nothing she said made any sense at all. 'I'm not hungry.'

After a time she accepted that he wanted to be left alone, and took the spurned food away. She wondered if she should stop preparing meals since no one ate them any more. She was throwing away more than was eaten.

Dave met her at the foot of the stairs. 'You can tell Scott from me that as soon as we can go out again, he's to leave. There's no place for him here. I should never have let him come back. He was right the first time. Farming's not for him.'

Linda put the plate down and stroked her husband's arm. 'Dave love, let it be for now. You're not thinking straight, we none of us are. Let's just do what has to be done and let the rest go. We'll only do and say things we regret otherwise.'

'Meaning I'll regret what I've just said? Oh no, Linda, I was never more sure about anything in all my life. Scott goes, the first moment he's allowed. That's all I have to say on the subject.'

Linda, full of anguish for them all, decided to let the matter rest for now. She went to load the dishwasher. Vicky was back in front of the television, watching *Casualty* with Jade beside her. Once the programme had finished they were despatched to bed, though Linda made a point of going up to tuck them in and kiss them goodnight. This, she felt, was a time when even Vicky might be glad to revert to childhood.

Linda and Dave sat up long into the night, sometimes talking over the practicalities of what was to come – their emotions were too painful for expression, or rather, they

49

were both still too numb with shock to know what they felt – and sometimes sitting in a gloomy silence. Dave said nothing more about his feelings towards Scott, and Linda thought it wiser not to bring the subject up again. Trying to ease the tension, she made hot drinks and piled a plate with chocolate biscuits, which she later had to return, untouched, to their tin. 'We'll get through it,' Linda kept saying, trying to convince herself as much as Dave. 'People did in 1967. And hopefully that was worse. They know so much more now.' But they neither of them found any comfort in the thought.

After about half an hour Dave suddenly got up from his seat by the fire. 'I'm going out.' Linda half rose to follow him but he held out a hand, repelling her. 'I want to be alone.'

Outside the hills glimmered with frosted snow. The air was cold, though it carried traces of smoke from two fires glowing in the valley, underlaid with a sickly stench. It was as well, Dave thought, that it was too cold for many smells to be carried. Then he found himself thinking that the ministry men would have a job tomorrow, digging a burial pit in the hard ground; maybe there'd be a pyre here too. He felt tears spring to his eyes – he who never cried, who had not even wept at his father's funeral! This evening he found that tears were dangerously close to the surface.

He moved away from the yard with its unforgiving security light, and into the darkness beyond, along the track that led to the field where he could hear the slight movements of the sleeping sheep, dimly make out their pale rounded shapes – his flock, cared for by his own hand, nurtured in the same way his father had done before him. Behind him, from the cow byre, came the occasional shuffle and stamping of feet. The cattle too were a part of his life, part of him. Out here, he was one with them, sharing this last night of their lives.

It was odd – he had taken sheep and cattle to market hundreds of times, and to the abattoir too; that was their purpose after all, to provide food and clothing. Yet always there had been the bulk of the flock or the herd left here at Middle Byers, a continuity stretching back far into the past. He had never dreamed there would come a time when there was nothing left. For that was what it would be: nothing.

He pressed the back of his hand to his mouth to keep back the sobs, groping in his pocket with the other for his cigarettes. Then, with a shock that the old instinct should still remain after all these years, he remembered that he'd given up, that it was a very long time since he'd had a packet of cigarettes anywhere within reach, let alone in his pocket. How could he have forgotten? It had been seven years ago now, after his father – still mourning the recent death of his mother – was diagnosed with the lung cancer that had killed him within weeks. But Dave would have smoked now, if he'd had the means, without hesitation. After all, what did his future health matter, when tomorrow he would lose everything that made life worthwhile, everything that made him what he was?

Instead, he leaned on the wall that bounded the field where the sheep grazed and stared out into the darkness, feeling, hearing, smelling, taking in for the last time with all his senses the things that would be gone tomorrow; the way of life that his son, in his careless disregard for his father's wishes, had so wilfully destroyed.

Upstairs in the farmhouse, in the bedroom they so resentfully shared, the girls were still awake. Vicky was raging against the fate which was to confine her to the farm for still more weeks to come, with no hope of seeing her friends, of doing any of the things that made life bearable. Normally, not being able to go to school would have been a cause for rejoicing, but not when it meant she couldn't do anything else instead. It was bad enough living on a farm miles from anywhere, with nothing to do and nothing within reach, so you had to negotiate for a lift whenever you wanted to go out, with no freedom to do anything as and when you chose. But all these things she so resented now seemed like untrammelled liberty set against the days that lay ahead. How would she be able to bear it?

There was a small sound from the bed at the other side of the room. She had thought Jade was asleep, but now she saw her sister sliding out of bed. She could just make her out, tiptoeing softly towards the door. She reached out and snapped on her bedside light; Jade swung round. Vicky saw then that she had pulled on a pair of jeans over her pyjamas, and a jumper. 'What are you doing?'

'I've got to go down to Polly. I've got to find a way to save her.'

All her own resentments fled. Vicky got out of bed and went to her sister. 'You can't, Jade. They think she's got the disease too. I heard the vet say so. There's nothing you can do. You shouldn't even go near her.' Jade gave a little whimpering cry and Vicky held her, stroking her hair. 'I tell you what,' she suggested. 'You can sleep in my bed tonight. This isn't a time to be alone.' Alongside a genuine compassion for her sister, Vicky had a sudden vision of herself as wise and mature, the consoler of her little sister, the person Jade could depend on in this crisis.

It worked too, for Jade allowed Vicky to lead her to bed and help her to undress again and the two of them lay side by side, the younger child in her sister's arms, where at last she fell asleep. Vicky stayed awake a little longer, with feelings that mingled a sense of her own generosity in sharing her bed – something she was rarely prepared to do – a sudden awareness of the drama of the situation, horrible though it was, and a real compassion for the younger girl and the loss she would soon be facing.

Some instinct she could not quite explain took Sally Oldfield to Meadhope parish church the following morning. Part of it was simply wanting to fill the time that stretched ahead without Ben and the farm. She also felt that it could, at the very least, do no harm to pray that everything would be all right, that they would come through this time unscathed. The final impulsion had been a call from Ben this morning, telling her that Middle Byers had been hit and that their own stock would now be rigorously tested until the ten days' incubation period was at an end. 'Don't worry too much, darling,' he'd said. 'Our animals are strong and healthy. They're in the best possible position to resist this disease.' She had sensed that he was trying to convince himself as much as her.

The service, holy communion for the first Sunday in Lent, chimed with her mood. She was glad that Rosalind included lengthy prayers for the farming community. Sally, who had for so long seen herself and Ben as rather outside that community – some of whom regarded them with a mixture of derision and contempt – now for the first time began to feel a member of it, linked in dread and horror. Though part of her still held on to a conviction that they were different, that if anyone at all was to blame for the outbreak, then they – organic farmers with their pure agricultural methods, their concern for the environment – could not be held responsible. Like Ben, she allowed herself to hope that their farming methods would enable their animals to keep clear of infection.

At the back of the church after the service, Rosalind asked Sally how she was, and sympathized warmly with the sadness of her self-imposed exile. 'If I can do anything to help, let me know. You know where I am. And you're all in my prayers.'

Sally thanked her; even if she were to make no use at all of the offer, the fact that it had been made – and sincerely so – was comforting. So, too, was the fact that when she returned to the guest house, expecting a solitary afternoon until her evening meal, she found that Elaine had prepared Sunday lunch – roast pork and all the trimmings – and expected Sally to join her and her daughter Lisa at the table. 'There's no way I'd let you eat alone. We'll just have a light supper tonight. Don't worry, there'll be no extra charge.'

That Sunday was more harrowing for the Emerson family than any of them could have imagined, though in an odd way it was also easier, because they all had things to do. Linda gave Scott the task of amusing his sisters, incarcerated in the living room that looked out over the fields from which all the animals had now been driven. Jolted out of his misery, Scott occupied them as best he could with card games, television, and some very loud music of Vicky's choice on the CD player. Even then they could hear the confused lowing and bleating as their parents rounded up the animals and drove them into the yard; and the muffled shots that followed, and seemed to go on for hours.

Perhaps worse was the silence that at the end of the day fell over the farm, rising like a miasma from the empty byres and the empty fields to wrap itself around them all.

Six

In the rectory garden, Rosalind was spending an hour of her day off weeding the overgrown bed by the front door, though it was cold and threatened snow again. There had been a long interregnum between the last rector's leaving and Rosalind's arrival, so there was a whole season's neglect to put right. The vigorous work soothed her restlessness a little. She longed to go for a good brisk walk, but there were so few places left *to* walk – only the main roads and built-up areas. So much for her plans and dreams!

As she uprooted a young dandelion, struggling with its already tenacious root, she thought of her telephone conversation with her father last night, when he had complained about the closed footpaths around their home, which seemed so unnecessary since there had been no outbreak of foot-and-mouth in the area. Then she had told him how it was in her parish, how every day brought new cases of the disease; how steadily, horribly, the fields and byres were being emptied, and he had been all troubled sympathy. 'It's difficult timing, when you're so new to the parish,' he had observed, echoing what she already felt. She needed so much to show that she cared – that God cared – for these people in their suffering, but she was still hardly established here, still only beginning to learn what normal life was like for her parishioners. Now, suddenly, nothing was normal any more.

'I just haven't managed to deal with it myself,' she'd admitted. 'I suppose I came here with all sorts of middle class preconceptions about bad farming methods, about the whole approach to farming by successive governments. I've been inclined to think that most farmers go along with it, that they're subsidy junkies who put profits before everything. I know that's what some people are saying, even here. There are a lot of incomers in the village itself, people like me, I suppose. There's quite a lot of talk about how the farmers have brought all this on themselves, which is nonsense, I know. I've met farmers and their families who are nothing like that – good, kind people who take a pride in what they do. Yet in a way I think I've more in common with the incomers than with the farmers. But I've got to find a way of understanding what it's like for farmers at the moment, otherwise I shall be no use at all.' She had heard the gentle murmur at the other end of the line that told her William Percival was listening intently. 'You must have found it hard sometimes, when we were at Little Combe – it was such a feudal place, not like Meadhope at all. There must have been people you didn't have much in common with.'

'*Anything* in common, a great many of them,' he'd agreed. 'On the surface at least. Yet we all have the one supreme thing – we are all children of the same heavenly father, brothers and sisters in Christ. Put that thought first, and the rest falls into place.'

'I know.' As she did, but it had been helpful to be reminded of it all the same. After a moment she'd continued, 'One thing I have learned is that farming round here is nothing like the agribusiness in most of the country. Farms are small and struggling; little traditional hill farms.'

'Not at all like Little Combe, then.'

'No. Maybe even big business farmers are distressed if they get hit by foot-and-mouth, but if it's your whole way of life, for generations, then it must be devastating. There are bad farmers, like that pig farmer at Heddon-on-the-Wall who seems to have started it all. But they're the minority. It's not only organic farmers who take a pride in their work, who love their animals, who even care about the environment. And I'm quite sure God's with them in their suffering, not judging them. After all, to blame them is to do exactly what people have done through the ages – to assume that suffering is a punishment for sin. I know that's not true.'

'Which is a hard thing to put across, the hardest part of being a parish priest – no matter where you are.' There had been a pause, then he'd said, 'You know you'll have our prayers, you and your parishioners.' She had found the thought comforting and ended the call feeling that she would be able to see her way through, that she would be shown the way. It was, after all, no bad thing that she should be forced to confront her own prejudices.

Overhead, she suddenly heard a long rippling call, magical in its sense of wildness, of remote places. She lifted her head to listen, recognizing what it was – a curlew, returned from its winter habitat to nest in this lovely hill country; returned for the spring. Whatever devastation might have desolated this land, something at least remained, some sound of hope and continuance. Its loveliness brought tears to her eyes.

Then a sharp scattering of snow stung her face so she went indoors. She found a message on the answerphone from Sophie. Her daughter had phoned to let her know she was planning to come home for Mothering Sunday, the weekend after next. Rosalind felt delighted – like the sound of the curlew, this was something to bring light into a difficult time. When Sophie had lived at home, the relationship between mother and teenage daughter had been as thorny as one would expect – as was normal. Now, they were the best of friends and Rosalind hugely enjoyed her company. She opened her organizer to make a note of the visit – not that she really needed such a reminder, but it somehow made it more concrete. Then she saw that she had a wedding booked for the Saturday of that weekend, for the marriage of a local solicitor to Julie Hall, daughter of a prominent farming family to the west of Meadhope, who had booked the date the day after her induction. Rosalind had duly read the banns, but it was time she got in touch to make the final arrangements – she was a little surprised that they had not already been made. Day off or not, as dusk fell, she thought this might be a good time to find someone at home as at least some of the family came in from their work on the farm. She rang the number, feeling a little apprehensive; after all, she might be trying to contact them just as they were finding foot-and-mouth in their animals. She knew the farm was not among those most recently listed as having been hit, but there were new cases every hour. On the other hand, perhaps the planning of a joyful family event would be giving them much needed solace in these grim times.

The male voice that eventually answered her call was impatient, hostile, suspicious. 'Yes?'

'This is Rosalind Maclaren, from Meadhope rectory,' she said. 'I wondered if we could meet to make arrangements for the wedding.'

'Wedding? While all this is going on? No way. We called it off weeks ago.'

Rosalind resisted the impulse to retort, 'You might have told me!' After all, they must have troubles enough without that. She sensed that to ask how things were with them would not be appreciated, so she simply said gently, 'Just let me know when you want to rearrange things,' and rang off.

At the dinner table that evening, talking over the day, Rosalind told Alastair of the postponed wedding. 'It brings home the devastation this outbreak's causing to the farmers. It's overturned everything – anything you might call normal life has been put on hold. It makes you wonder if things can ever get back to normal once it's over.'

'I suppose they will, eventually. It doesn't show much sign of letting up for now, does it? What have we got – outbreaks in Northumberland, Cumbria, here of course, and then all over the West Country and Wales too? Not good. I wonder if they'll put off the election?' Council elections were due to take place on May 3rd, and it had been assumed that the general election would soon be officially announced for the same day. 'I can't see canvassing going down too well while everyone's so jumpy about unnecessary moving about. Oh, talking of which – we had a discussion last night about cancelling choir practices.'

'What did you decide?'

'Most members come from the village, so we thought we'd keep going. Some people have already dropped out anyway – Linda Emerson from Middle Byers, of course. But I can't see how the rest of us are going to spread foot-and-mouth by singing together once a week. On the other hand, there's the question of our concert. Will we get anyone coming to hear us, the way things are? Should we even try to encourage them?'

'You may get fewer people, but does that matter? Though I suppose cancelling shows a kind of solidarity with the farmers.' Rosalind took a few more mouthfuls of mushroom risotto. 'I tell you what, how about putting on the concert on Palm Sunday evening, in church? I'll say evensong beforehand, for anyone who wants it, then we can have the concert at the usual evensong time, six o'clock. It would have a certain appropriateness about it. We could have a collection for the farmers' hardship fund.'

'A good idea. That would seem about right. I'll put it to everyone next week.'

'I'll have to put it to the PCC too, I think, just to keep everyone happy. But I can't see a problem.'

'Now where have I heard that before?' mused Alastair.

Rosalind laughed. 'All the times before I've found there was a great big problem, I know. And I'm still feeling my way with this PCC of course. I'm not even a hundred per cent sure of all their names yet. But we can hope for the best.'

The familiar animal smells that had been part of life at Middle Byers since it was built had been wiped away as if they had never been. The smell of disinfectant hung in the air, filling the byres and outbuildings from the moment the decontamination began. It seemed to fill the house too, seeping into every corner, and into the mouths and nostrils of all who lived there.

On the very day that their quarantine ended, Dave took steps to set in motion what he saw as another kind of essential disinfection. For the first time in ten days he made a point of coming into the kitchen while Scott was eating his breakfast. The boy put his spoon down, reddening. 'Dad—'

'I hope you've packed your bags.'

'Dad, please—'

'Your sisters go back to school today. School bus comes at eight thirty. I want you gone by then too. I don't care how, but I don't want to set eyes on you again. I've enough reminders of what's happened without you being under my feet.'

At that moment Linda came into the kitchen to collect the girls' packed lunches from the fridge. She halted in the doorway, looking in dismay from her son's anguished face to her husband's merciless one and back again. 'What's going on?'

'Scott's just leaving. I'm checking he's got everything packed.'

Scott stood up, sending his chair clattering on to the stone floor behind him. 'Dad, I never meant . . . you know I—'

'All I know is—'

Linda clung to her husband's arm. 'Dave, you can't do this! You'll never forgive yourself, believe me!'

He shook her off, turning to face her. 'What I can never forgive is that I ever let him come home. He's no son of mine, nor ever will be.' He swung back to the lad. 'Now, get moving, before I have to throw you out with my own hands.'

If Scott paused at all to wonder how easily his father – sturdier than he, but no taller and a good deal older – might be able to carry out his threat, he showed no sign of it. He left the room, ran upstairs, and within half an hour had ridden away on his motorbike. His mother managed to catch him before he left, just long enough to say, 'You've got my mobile number, and I've got yours. Let me know where you are and what you're doing. I'll talk your dad round, I promise.'

'You'll be lucky,' said Scott bitterly, and set the bike in motion. He didn't hear his mother's final 'I love you!'

spoken just before Dave, angry that she should be showing any sort of favour to the son he'd disowned, came to drag her back into the farmhouse. Linda's only tiny feeling of relief was for the fact that the girls had not seen or heard any of what was going on – at least not as far as she could tell.

But she was furious with Dave, not least because she was certain that he would come bitterly to regret what had happened. 'Have you thought what's going to become of Scott? Where's he going to go?'

Dave shrugged. 'It's up to him. Back to the town, where he belongs. You always said he'd never want for a job. So long as it's not here I don't care.'

'And what will you do when we come to restock? There'll be a massive amount of work – you'll need all the help you can get.'

Dave's reaction shocked her like a blast of freezing air. 'Restock? You don't think I'm going to risk going through all this again, do you? No, this farm's finished. Soon as we've got through the clearing up, once the epidemic's finally over – if that day ever comes – then we're selling up.' And at that he left her, whistling to Bess to follow as he crossed the empty yard. Far in the distance, the long rippling call of a curlew echoed over the empty fields.

Scott felt as if he were choking inside his helmet as he roared down the hill towards Meadhope. He drove instinctively, scarcely knowing where he was going, with no clear thought as to what he was going to do. He only knew that he hurt, with a terrible wrenching pain that was compounded by grief and loss and guilt and had no remedy.

In Meadhope he halted in a corner of the empty car park near the recreation ground – no one was coming to the dale these days unless they had to, and in any case it was early on a working day. He climbed off the bike and sat down at one of the picnic tables and stared into space, trying to make his mind focus on the immediate future. What was he going to do? Where could he go now? He had friends from his school days in the village, but they would all be at work at this time

61

of day, so he could hardly turn to any of them, or not for the moment. This evening, perhaps, though he shrank inwardly at the prospect of explaining why he had so suddenly found himself homeless, especially as he'd already told most of them how happy he was to be home . . .

There was Lisa of course – he glanced in the direction of Rose Cottage. She might be at home, if today was one of the days when she had no lectures. He rather thought so, but couldn't remember clearly; his brain didn't seem to be functioning properly. But it was such a new relationship. Their first proper date should have taken place on that dreadful evening when Armstrongs' had been hit by the disease. They had talked on the phone since; she had seemed sympathetic and still warm towards him, but he could not be sure. It had been such a stormy relationship right from the start, from the moment when he first saw her in the pub in Darlington, sitting among her friends at the next table.

He had been with a group from work, drivers and mechanics. It was last September, during the fuel protests, which the firm he worked for had supported with enthusiasm, supplying pickets for fuel depots, joining go-slows on motorways. They had been talking of tactics, of the dramatic effect their action had already had – causing panic buying of fuel and then rationing, with long queues at petrol stations. A few days more and the entire country would be brought to a standstill; the government would have to listen. Fuel taxes would be slashed, and people power would have won. He had said little, simply listened, but not very closely, for he was watching Lisa who was in animated conversation with her friends. In her close-fitting black tee shirt, every sweet curve of her was amply visible; her perfect legs stretched below her brief flowery skirt. Then she turned his way and with one glance of her wide blue eyes he knew he was hers for ever. He could not believe it when she suddenly came over; he thought she was about to say something to him, something in reponse to what he felt. Instead she began to argue with his friends, telling them – and him as well – that they should be ashamed of themselves, that fuel taxes stopped the environment being more damaged than it was already, that even high as they were they came nowhere near to paying for the damage that road transport cost the country. She argued eloquently, fiercely, with a passion that made her face glow, her eyes shine. Then she sat down beside him and turned her gaze on him alone. 'Tell me, have you ever really thought about what you're doing?'

The answer to that had to be no, though he did not say it. He had simply gone along with what his mates were doing; it seemed unarguable that right was on their side. But he had never been given to thinking much about any issue. Now, he remembered one argument he had heard put forward, which had stuck in his mind as being rather different from the usual ones. 'If they want more taxes, they should raise income tax,' he said. 'That's the fair way to go. That way, it's only people who can afford it who pay.'

To his amazement, it worked – for a moment anyway. She faltered, gazed at him with increased attention, and then smiled the most enchanting smile he had ever seen in all his life. 'You've got a point there.' His heart leapt. 'But still, that doesn't help the environment.' Oh well, he had tried; just for a moment he had gained her interest, even her approval.

'Can I get you a drink?' he heard himself saying; she had left a glass behind on her table, but it was empty. He had not really expected her to accept his offer.

'Thanks,' she'd said, to his amazement. So he had bought her a half pint of lager and they sat talking as if no one else was there.

But that had not been the beginning, not really. After that, they would meet from time to time in one pub or another, sometimes by pre-arrangement, sometimes by chance. He would think he saw every sign that she was attracted to him, then he would make some apparently innocuous remark and everything would fall apart. He would, for instance, mention that before he left home, he sometimes used to get work as a beater for one of the local shoots, a seasonal money-earner which he also enjoyed; and she would turn on him with a vehement tirade against all blood sports. She didn't seem to include fishing in the scope of her disapproval, at which he accused her of disliking only what supposed 'posh' people did in their leisure time, an argument that had enraged her and for a whole week caused her to avoid him altogether. And then it had apparently all blown over, for he found her sitting alone in her usual pub the next time he went in, and she had greeted him as if there had never been any disagreement between them. Slowly, cautiously, he had tried to build up to asking her out for a proper date and then, just before Christmas, she had announced she was moving. For just a moment his heart felt as if it had tumbled through the floor – until she told him her mother was buying an old house in Meadhope to convert into a guest house.

That announcement coincided with his own growing discontentment with town life, which Christmas at home had simply crystallized. Lisa's move to the village had finally made up his mind for him. He had come home, begun to feel as if he had never been away, though with all the restlessness of the past wiped out; he knew he had done the right thing in returning to farming. Better still, Lisa had been so openly delighted to find that he was living nearby that he could no longer have any doubts about her feelings for him. And then, just when it looked as though things were going his way, this horrible disease had blasted into his life, shattering everything.

Could he go to Rose Cottage and see if Lisa was there? Might she offer him a roof over his head? There was plenty of space in the house, he knew that – he had been back with her one evening a few weeks ago, and got as far as kissing her in the empty visitors' lounge. But the place was a guest house, and he could not afford to pay anything, or not at least until he was working again.

That settled it, of course. He must go back to work. He had no idea if Armstrongs' was back in business – he had not wanted to get in touch with them while he was at home, since they had been the cause of him destroying his father's life's work. Now was the moment to find out. At least if he could go back to work he would be able to pay something towards his accommodation, wherever it might be.

He got on his bike again and drove to the small industrial estate at the end of the village, to Armstrongs' yard. It certainly didn't look like a thriving business, though the gate stood open on to the silent expanse of tarmac. He parked his bike and wandered about the workshops and garages looking for any sign of life, anyone to speak to. Finding no one, he went to the office where Kelly, with whom he'd been at school, sat talking to Mike Armstrong, the boss. Mike turned and said, 'Scott! How's things?'

'We're in the clear now,' he said. The words sounded hollow; what possible meaning could they have, when nothing was left? 'Just wondered when I could start back to work.'

'Sorry, lad. Nothing doing. Business is terrible. Maybe in a month or two, if things show signs of picking up. But for now – well, you can see for yourself how it is.'

He could see clearly enough, but it was still thoroughly disheartening. He left, trying not to let his depression show. What now? Some cold little voice in his head said, 'Back to Darlington.' He would find work there, he knew that. But to go back to what he had left so hopefully just over a month ago – and to go back without having made things up with his father – would feel like a defeat. Yet what choice was there?

He had enough money for a coffee at the small teashop in the market place. He rode back there and parked. As he got off his bike he saw Lisa, a radiance emerging from the nearby supermarket. 'Hi!' she said, though her eyes and her smile seemed to say much more. 'They've let you out again then?'

When she reached him he said baldly, 'Turned me out, you mean.'

She listened, appalled, as he told her what had happened. 'That's awful!' The way she caressed his arm made his head spin. 'What are you going to do?'

'Go back to Darlington, I suppose.'

At that point Lisa took charge of him completely. 'Oh, but you can't do that! Look, our house is just about empty – no guests at all, except Sally Oldfield. You can stay with us. Just till you sort things out with your father. He's got to come round soon, hasn't he?'

And so he found himself installed in the one small single room at Rose Cottage, on the floor below Lisa's own room, and being plied with coffee and wholehearted sympathy in the kitchen. He sensed that Lisa's mother was less than happy at having a non-paying guest inflicted upon her at this difficult time, but Lisa was very persuasive. 'It's only till he gets things sorted out with his dad. We can't let him sleep on the streets, can we?' So he stayed, and that evening Lisa came to his room and offered him the only comfort that could have reached him at this time.

Linda had managed to speak to Scott briefly on his mobile, phoning from work during her lunch break, and was reassured to know he was, for the time being, safe and well. In fact, he sounded rather happier than she had expected him to be in the circumstances, though their conversation ended with the inevitable question to which she had no clear answer. 'Do you think Dad will come round?'

She tried at intervals during the following days to get Dave to talk about his son, to consider relenting, but the moment she brought the subject up, Dave would snarl at her or simply walk away. She felt helpless. She was angry that he should be so intransigent, yet at the same time understood what was making him behave like this and wished she could do something to ease the desperate pain that was at the bottom of it. She shared his pain of course, but she had never been as closely bound up with the farm as he was. He had been born and raised here, worked for years alongside his father, lived through good times and bad – though never as bad as this. More to the point, for her the central focus of her life had always been the people, not the animals; the children, and Dave himself.

At first, he would not even give his attention to completing the sheaf of forms necessary for claiming compensation for the lost animals. To everyone's astonishment it was Vicky who found a way out of that dilemma. Coming into the kitchen one evening she heard her mother nagging her father on just this matter. 'You promised to make a start on it today. Dave, we need the money, you know we do!'

'What for? We're finished.'

'We still need to eat, Dad.' Both her parents looked round in astonishment at their daughter. 'I tell you what,' she went on, just like a bossy mother, 'I'll give you a hand. We'll do them together, after supper.'

Perhaps Dave was too amazed at his daughter's offer – and her manner – to refuse, for he merely said, 'OK then.' After the meal he went meekly to the office with Vicky and spent several hours laboriously working at the individual certificates that had to be filled out for each one of his beloved animals. Once the claim was sent in, he seemed calmer than he had been for weeks. Linda did not risk asking him if he still wanted to sell up, nor – even more problematic – if he might consider relenting towards his son, but she began at last to hope that they might be over the very worst. She could have hugged Vicky, but sensed that her daughter wanted to assume the mantle of responsible adulthood without comment or display. This astonishing transformation was the one unequivocally good thing to come from the ghastliness of the past days. She clung to it as a sign of hope, an indication that other good things too might emerge one day, if she had both patience and tenacity.

Seven

'What are you getting your mam for Mother's Day?' Lisa asked on Saturday morning, as she and Scott lingered over breakfast in the kitchen at Rose Cottage.

'How can I get anything? I'm not going to see her, am I?'

'You saw her last week.' Linda had called at the guest house after work to spend some time with her son. It did not seem to have done much to cheer Scott; on the contrary, he seemed more depressed than ever at the continuing rift with his father.

'Haven't any money, have I?'

'You could manage a card, surely? I'll lend you the cash if you like.'

'Too late for the post now.'

Lisa felt a rush of impatience – not for the first time during the past weeks. In fact, she was becoming increasingly irritated by Scott's inaction as she saw it. He had, it was true, made some attempt to find work in Meadhope, but there was nothing available. None of the local garages had need of mechanics; pubs were cutting back on staff due to lack of custom; the village's few small shops had all the staff they needed, and were also missing the tourist trade that usually began to increase their incomes at this time of year. It was not Scott's fault that things were so difficult, and she did not really want him to have to look further afield for work. But she knew how hard things were for her mother, who had reluctantly taken Scott in and ten days later was still having to feed him, without any payment at all. If he could not find work in Meadhope, and his father would

68

not have him back home, then it was tough, but he had to steel himself to move back to Darlington or somewhere else where work was available. She could see that, even if he couldn't. She sat looking at his lean, handsome face, marred with sullen misery, and wondered if she could go on loving him if he didn't make some sort of effort to snap out of his present inertia.

'Oh well,' she said. 'The offer's there if you change your mind.' She stood up. 'I'm going out to get some flowers. I've got Mam some of her favourite perfume already, but it wouldn't be Mother's Day without flowers, would it?' She had used up two weeks' worth of the allowance her mother gave her on the gift, but did not regret it one bit. Her mother needed pampering for a change.

As she turned to go, leaving Scott gloomily chewing on a final slice of toast – depression did not seem to have affected his appetite – Sally came into the room. 'Have I missed breakfast? I didn't mean to be so late.'

She looked terrible, Lisa thought, her eyes set in bruise-coloured shadows; they had a dazed expression, as if she were not quite sure where she was and why. 'I thought you'd had yours,' Lisa said. 'Mam's upstairs. I can do you something.'

'That's all right. I'm fine with toast – I can do it myself.'

Lisa filled the kettle. 'I'll make coffee.' She glanced round. 'Are you OK?'

Sally sat down suddenly. 'Yes, I'm fine.'

That, Lisa thought, was an obvious lie. She wondered if there'd been bad news from Sally's husband back at the farm, but did not like to ask. With Scott in the room she didn't want to talk about foot-and-mouth disease, even obliquely. Things were bad enough already. On the other hand, she didn't feel she could abandon Sally to Scott's cheerless company, so she lingered in the kitchen, making coffee and toast, clearing away dirty dishes, filling the dishwasher.

Sally began to eat, but after a couple of mouthfuls came

69

to a halt and pushed her plate away. 'I don't seem to be hungry after all.' She looked close to tears.

Elaine's return to the kitchen sent Scott on his way; he could sense her disapproval and avoided her as much as possible. He went to sit in his room, watching whatever was on the small portable television. Lisa set out for the shops, leaving the two older women together.

It was then that it came out. 'You look as if you've had a bad night,' Elaine said, and saw Sally's face crumple with misery.

'Ben called my mobile. He'd just had Jack Sheffield on the phone, from Low Intake, to tell him his cows were down and the ministry men were on their way up to us.'

She had known Ben was phoning her from the study and could see him there as he spoke, imagine the lines etched by anguish on his face. The study was the one room that was filled with all the things that marked Moor Farm out as something different from the traditional farm such as any intruder from a past century would have recognized; the one room that linked them with their past life, before they had given up everything for their dream. There were two computers, the printer and scanner, the fax machine, and the manuals on many aspects of animal husbandry that had guided them during the years of learning and struggling. Behind Ben, as he stood by the window where the phone was kept, a light would blink here and there, or a whirring and clicking would indicate the arrival of a fax; on Ben's screen the marching chickens he had jokingly designed as a screen saver would be shifting lazily over the surface. She could see it all as clearly as if she were there with him, while her heart seemed to come to a stop inside her for whole minutes at a time.

'Have his cows been in contact with yours then?' Elaine asked.

Sally shook her head. 'You know this new contiguous cull they've just announced? Every animal within a three-kilometre radius of an outbreak has to be culled – even if there's been no possible contact, even if they're fields away.'

'Even if they're not sick?'

Sally nodded, not trusting herself to speak. The worst thing of all was to know that Ben was going to have to face all the coming horror alone, without her support and companionship. 'I'm coming home!' she had said to him this morning, but he had protested vehemently. Now, if ever, she must stay away, look after herself, try and forget what was happening. If she came home he would wish he hadn't told her the news, and would think twice before telling her anything else. So she had agreed; but now she laid her head on the table and burst into tears. 'I want to go home – yet I don't!'

Elaine sat down beside her and put her arms round her. 'I know, I know. But think of the baby – think of the future! Things will be better, one day. By the time the baby comes it'll all be over and you'll have forgotten it ever happened.'

'And what about Ben? What will it do to him?'

That was a difficult one. Elaine thought hard for a moment, then said, 'Won't he think he has to get through it for you, for the baby? If he hadn't got the baby to look forward to, it would be much worse, wouldn't it?'

'I suppose so.' But all Sally could think of now was the births that would never happen. There would be no lambing this year at Moor Farm.

Both Sophie and Josh came home to the rectory for Mothering Sunday, arriving on the Friday night. It was the first time either of them had been with their mother for the celebration since they had become students; even longer since they had all been together for the day. Rosalind was delighted and touched, though she recognized that the chief reason was probably the attraction of Meadhope itself.

But if it was partly the beauty of the place that had brought them to Meadhope, then it was obvious they immediately began to realize that things were not as they had been when they had last seen the place. 'What's that horrible stink?'

Josh asked as he got out of the car, when his father had collected him from the station.

'Pyres for sheep and cattle,' said Alastair grimly. 'Welcome to the countryside.'

Sophie, of course, did not need to ask. As a vet nearing the end of her training, she was only too aware of what was happening. Over breakfast the following morning she said, 'They're starting to talk about bringing in trainees like me to help with the outbreak. There's such a desperate shortage of vets.'

'What would that involve?' Rosalind asked; she had just returned from saying mattins to find that Alastair had produced bacon and eggs all round. Even Josh had dragged himself out of bed as soon as the savoury odours reached him.

'Looking for symptoms, of course. But probably killing animals too. I just hope they get the outbreak under control soon, before they get round to it. That's not why I became a vet. The odd one now and then, yes, but not this mass slaughter.'

'Do you understand why they don't vaccinate? There seem to be all sorts of views about it. Would vaccination work?'

'Yes, of course. They're using it in Holland already. But it makes exporting meat more difficult.'

'So it's to do with trade and money,' Rosalind continued, 'not animal welfare as such?'

'It is, but then if you think about it that's why farmers keep animals anyway, so you have to take it into account.'

'Do *you* think they should vaccinate?'

'I really don't know. I'm not an expert in that field and there seem to be so many conflicting views. But in any case, unless you get the Farmers' Union backing it, you couldn't really do it anyway.'

'Right!' said Alastair, standing up and beginning to stack the empty plates. 'That's enough about death and disease. What do you folks want to do today?'

Outside, it was raining, the sort of morning when it barely

got light. 'Stoke up the fire and settle down with the papers?' suggested Sophie.

'I've got some work still to do on tomorrow's service,' Rosalind said. 'But it shouldn't take long. We could have lunch at the Black Horse if you like. They'll probably be glad of the custom.'

'I could do with some fresh air,' Josh said. 'Anyone fancy a walk?'

No one did. His mother said, 'Keep to main roads, Josh. And keep away from animals.'

'And bring an *Echo* back with you,' his father added.

Josh was glad no one wanted to join him; he enjoyed solitary walks, finding them good times for thinking, or – more often – simply clearing his head. Today his head was already clear, and it was cold and cheerless, but he walked briskly up the hill out of the village, keeping to the road as he had been warned to do. It was better up here, out of reach of the smoke that lay in a sickly pall over the valley. He could see no signs here of burning or slaughter. There were even some animals peacefully grazing in the fields. He began to feel better as he always did at times like this, losing the awkwardness, the sense of being uncomfortably different that had burdened him for as long as he could remember. Among his fellow students, he tried to blend in by drinking as hard as the others did, by being one of the lads, but it was always an effort, made possible only with copious amounts of alcohol. It was good to be at home where everyone accepted him just as he was; except that on the whole he didn't much like who he was. He felt as if there must be someone more acceptable, more desirable, another kind of person that he could become. Out here, alone, he began to feel strong, virile, confident, though he knew that as soon as he found himself amongst others again he would be once more the boy who had to make a constant strenuous effort to appear to have any personality at all.

Passing a small plantation of trees, he came upon a field with lambs skipping about, tugging at their mothers' udders, waggling their long untidy tails. They looked so normal, so delightful, that he paused to watch, leaning on the wall. Twin lambs nearby stopped chasing each other and came over to stare at him. 'Hello, littl'uns!' he greeted them. He reached out a hand.

There was a sudden noise, a shout, then a sharp crack, and something whistled past his head, just missing him. He put up a hand to his hair, stared across the field, and saw a furious figure in the lane beyond, jumping up and down with rage and aiming a gun at him – a gun! So that was what had just missed him!

Terror seized him and he turned and ran. It was only when he was well down the hill, far out of sight of that terrifying figure, that he stopped running and allowed the anger he felt to take shape. What sort of place was this, where some maniac could take a potshot at him? The police must be informed as soon as possible, but first he went home to tell his mother and see if she might know who was responsible.

He rushed into the house, pushing open the study door. 'Mum!'

Rosalind looked up from her desk. 'Good walk? What's the matter?' He told her, and she listened gravely, but when she spoke at last he was astonished by her response. 'You idiot, Josh. We told you to keep right away from any animals.'

'I did. I only talked to them.'

'You said you were leaning on the wall. That isn't keeping away.'

'But I've not got foot-and-mouth. Humans can't get it, can they?'

'Maybe not, but they may be able to spread it if they've been near infected animals. No one seems very sure – and the farmer certainly doesn't know that.'

'But still – to shoot at me!'

'I know, that was going much too far. Though I imagine he was only trying to scare you off.'

'He did that all right!'

He began to sense his mother's impatience at the interruption, and went to the sitting room in search of his father and sister, who were working through the various sections of the Saturday *Guardian*. 'You'll never believe what happened to me!' he announced. They looked up, and he told them.

They were as unsympathetic as his mother had been. 'You're a pillock,' said Sophie. 'Just imagine what it's like for the farmers, not knowing who's going to be hit next, not even sure what makes the infection spread so fast. They're jumpy as hell, and so would you be.'

'But a gun! That's grotesque! Even if he only meant to scare me, what if he'd missed – or rather, not missed? Don't tell me he'd get away with that!'

'Maybe not, but he wouldn't be thinking rationally. You need to put yourself in his shoes. He's afraid of losing everything, just because some idiot townie thinks his lambs look sweet.'

'I'm not an idiot townie!'

'Yes you are. Coldwell's a town, and that's where you grew up. You've got a townie mentality.'

'And where did you grow up then? You're as much a townie as I am.'

'But I've spent time working in the country, at country things, with country people. I've made an effort to listen and learn, which is more than you have.'

'Children, children!' Alastair broke in. 'Let's call a truce, shall we? Josh made a mistake, but there's no harm done.'

'*I* made a mistake! What about the farmer?'

'Oh, shut up, Josh,' said his sister. She changed the subject. 'Did you remember to get an *Echo*?'

He had not, so, seeking peace, he set out for the news-agents. There was a long queue at the counter – it was Saturday, the day of the main lottery draw, and everyone seemed to be buying last-minute tickets along with their papers. He tagged on behind the last person in the queue, a curvaceous girl with a tangled mass of brown hair, who glanced round at him once and then turned again to smile. 'Long wait this morning,' she said.

She was pretty, Josh noted with a lift of the spirits, with large blue eyes in a heart-shaped face, and a wide sensual mouth, whose smile seemed to fill the room. What was more, she seemed to be trying to strike up a conversation with him. The only trouble was, he couldn't think of anything sensible or significant to say in response. 'Yes, it is, isn't it?' was all he managed, accompanying it with a broad smile, which he hoped would compensate for his lack of wit or profundity. With an effort, he managed another contribution. 'I suppose in hard times people are more likely to pin their hopes on a win.' He wished he'd kept silent. He could see other people in the queue giving him odd looks, as if they wondered who that pretentious git was – and he did sound both pretentious and patronising, even to his ears. The girl too stopped smiling and looked thoughtful. He could imagine her thoughts, felt himself blushing and wished he could rewind to the moment he took up his place in the queue and start again. Instead, he'd blown it. 'Sorry,' he heard himself say. 'I'm having a bad day myself.'

'Better buy a lottery ticket then,' she suggested. 'Your luck might change.'

It was a thought. Perhaps the presence of the girl – the fact that she did not, after all, appear to have written him off yet – meant that his luck was indeed about to change. He felt in his pocket and found he barely had enough cash even to buy the paper. 'I'm skint,' he said. 'Typical student.' Inadvertently, he seemed to have found the key to a proper conversation, to an exchange of the sort of personal information that might lead on to something else.

'Tell me about it! I'm a student too. Environmental Studies at Teesside.'

'Computer Technology at Leicester.'

'Wow! Impressive. Then you're home for the weekend?'

Should he tell her where home was? He'd learned long ago how easily his background could put people off; not yet perhaps. 'Yes.'

'We're new to Meadhope, so I don't know many people yet.'

'We?' His heart thudded. Was she spoken for already, living with a boyfriend?

'Mam and me. Rose Cottage Guest House. We moved in just after Christmas. Two lots of guests so far, back in February – there were other bookings, but they all cancelled because of foot-and-mouth.'

'That's tough. Let's hope it's over soon.'

'Doesn't show much sign so far.' The man in front of her had been served and she moved forward to pay for the card she'd chosen from the rack at the far end of the shop. When it came to his turn, Josh noticed with delight that she had paused on her way to the door. Was she waiting for him?

She was, for she smiled as he reached her and fell into step alongside as he left the shop. 'I'm going this way.' She gestured along the street.

'So am I.' He knew he would have said that even if she had indicated quite the opposite direction. With regret, he saw that Rose Cottage Guest House was only a few yards away, on the corner of the lane that led up towards the church and the rectory. He'd never noticed it before, but now admired its neat stone exterior, the narrow beds bright with spring bulbs that fronted it, spilling their cheerful colour on to the pavement.

Then came the inevitable question. 'Where do you live?'

He took a deep breath and risked the truth. 'Up there. My mother's the rector.'

'Oh, right! She seems nice. If anyone could get me to go to church, it would be someone like her.'

Huge relief! Josh grinned and took another risk. 'Maybe you'd like to go out for a drink some time?'

'Maybe,' she said. It was not encouraging, though he tried to tell himself it was not a complete rejection. What was worse, they had reached the guest house and she was turning away from him, with a wave at once friendly and casual. 'See you!'

He watched her go into the house with a mixture of hope and despondency. It could have been worse, he told himself as he walked up the lane. She could have said, 'I don't think so,' in that final way he had come to know all too well from other girls he had approached. In a way, she had left a door open, so to speak. On the other hand, perhaps she was just a naturally friendly girl. 'Oh well,' he told himself. 'Can't win them all.' In any case, he was off back to Leicester again on Monday, and wouldn't be home again until Easter. It was just possible that he might then make some progress with the girl from Rose Cottage.

The following morning, Sally Oldfield appeared in church again. 'I thought seeing all the children with their gifts would make me feel more hopeful,' she said to Rosalind as she paused in the porch after the service. 'You know, our child will be doing this one day – that sort of thing.'

'But it hasn't worked,' suggested Rosalind gently; she could see that tears were not far away.

Sally explained what had happened at Moor Farm. 'They slaughtered the animals yesterday. Ben didn't tell me much, but he said it was horrible, worse than he could have imagined.'

Rosalind held her hand and listened with great sympathy. 'It must be very hard for you both, especially being apart like this. It seems so unfair too!'

To keep the tears at bay, Sally began to generalize. 'The whole thing's unfair, I suppose, for everyone. I'm lucky not to be in the middle of it. It's Ben I'm worried about. Farming's always been a bit of a solitary business, but now . . . Well, every farm's cut off, with nowhere to go, no social life, no contact with anyone, except by phone or email.'

Walking home a little later with Alastair, Rosalind told him what Sally had said. 'It struck me – it's just when people need the church most that we can't reach them. We're going to have to do something. We've got to find a way to show that we're there for those who want our help.'

'Services on the Internet, perhaps,' said Alastair with a grin. Rosalind came to a halt and he said quickly, 'Sorry, I know it's not funny. I shouldn't be making a joke—'

'No, no, it's not a joke. That could be the answer – one answer anyway. I'd need help setting it up. And we should make it ecumenical, to cater for all denominations. I wonder if John Parker has good computer skills? Otherwise – well, perhaps Sally would like to help? It would give her something to do. Then there's the other thing – all those isolated people, without any human interaction. Some of them at least will want someone to talk to, someone who'll listen and give advice if they need it, but mostly just listen. I wonder how one goes about setting up a telephone helpline?'

'Dear me, we are getting all high-tech! This doesn't quite sound like the traditional country parson you were going to be.'

'The world's changed. We have to use the means that are to hand. It makes sense.' She began to walk on again, more briskly. 'I'll phone John Parker and arrange a meeting.' She saw that Alastair looked puzzled. 'You know – Methodist minister, young, with a beard.'

'I know. But you're surely not going to phone him now?'

'Why not? We clergy don't look on Sunday as a day off, you know.'

'Leave it for one day, Rosie! Have you forgotten, our offspring are cooking the dinner?'

'All right. I'll choose my moment at least – no spoiling the festivities, I promise.' She reached up to push open the front door of the rectory. 'Mm! Good smells!'

At Middle Byers, Mother's Day brought Linda breakfast in bed, carried to her on a tray by Vicky and a whispering, giggling Jade. There were flowers too, and cards, but nothing at all from Scott. That absence made her heart ache and cast a shadow over the day. When Dave kissed her and told her, almost in his old warm tones, that she was the best mother in the world, she wanted to retort that she needed Scott to be there too if she was to feel truly loved. But she held back, fearing to sour Dave's mood and spoil what was good about this day.

She was told to get up when she was ready and then spend

the morning pleasing herself, while the others cooked the dinner. The trouble with that was that she was not used to pleasing herself and did not really know what to do. There was nothing she wanted to watch on television and they did not get Sunday papers; as for books, she was not much of a reader. It was a cold, damp day, so there was no encouragement to go outside – besides, the empty fields were too grim a reminder of what they had so recently lost. In the end, Vicky lent her a collection of old teenage magazines which she browsed through in a desultory way as she lounged on the living-room sofa. She did not quite like to admit, even to herself, that she was bored.

The phone rang mid-morning. She heard Dave answer it; a moment of silence, then an abrupt 'We've nothing to say to you!' She knew then who it must have been. She flung down the magazines and went out to catch Dave.

'Was that Scott?'

The smiling, tender Dave of this morning had given way to the morose and scowling man she had grown only too used to. 'You know what I said. He's no son of mine.'

'But he's my son and it's Mother's Day. Don't I have any say? I want to speak to him.'

Something in her tone must have conveyed the anguish she felt, and her anger that Dave should have been so dismissive of Scott's call. He gazed at her for a little time then said, 'You phone him back then.'

So she did, though it was not a very satisfactory call. Scott had obviously been hurt and thrown off balance by his father's reception. 'I thought you would answer,' he said. 'I didn't expect Dad.' He sounded miserable. She longed to be able to tell him to come home, to say he would be welcome at the Mother's Day dinner, but she knew that was impossible while Dave felt as he did. Mother and son talked a little longer, long enough for her to gather – as she knew already – that he had still not found a job, that he was giving up hope, but that he was otherwise well. He apologized for not sending a card or flowers, but he had no money. She guessed that even his relationship with Lisa

80

was suffering because of his unhappiness. She felt helpless and not much consoled by the call, except that she was glad that he had at least thought to ring.

Dave had mellowed again by the time the family sat down to eat, but only towards Linda. The meal was good and she was grateful for the effort they had all made. She let them wash up, though she itched to be doing something rather than just sitting about. Fortunately, once the washing up was done, things somehow returned to normal, without anything being said. It was Linda who got the tea while the girls occupied themselves in their usual Sunday afternoon manner – Vicky chattering on her mobile and playing music, Jade drawing a picture and doing some sewing. They still shared a bedroom because Linda refused to acknowledge that Scott was not coming back. In this she was adamant, as adamant as Dave was that Scott had gone for good. She too could be stubborn.

That evening, as she and Dave sat in silence in front of the television – there was nothing else to do at the end of the day, with the disinfection more or less complete and no animals but Bess to feed – Dave said suddenly, 'You know, Linda, I thought we were going to be all right. Scott was back, things were picking up, this place was worth working for. Just one thing wasn't right – Scott taking that job. Now that one thing's wrecked everything. There'll be no Emersons on this farm after us. My guess is some big businessman will buy it up, farm the land at long distance, and then sell off the house to rich townies who don't even work in the dale.'

'Not if we don't sell,' Linda pointed out. 'Not if we restock and carry on.'

'What's the point, with no one to take over?'

'That didn't seem to be a problem before Scott came home.'

'We still had animals then.'

Linda thought it would perhaps have been wiser not to say anything more, but she had put the subject aside so often while the rift between father and son gnawed at her all the time. She drew a deep breath and ventured, 'You know Scott meant no harm. He's as sorry as you are about what happened—'

'How can he be? If he had farming in his blood like he says, he'd have listened to me, not kept on with that job.'

'Oh Dave, you're being unfair! After all, it wasn't because of a risk of infection you didn't want him to take it – it was only because you thought there was enough work for him to do here—'

'As there was!'

'Maybe, but our income has never matched the amount of work. Scott was doing what he thought was best for all of us. In fact, I thought it was the right thing too, at the time. We weren't to know—'

'You! You thought it was the right thing! Then you encouraged him to go against me!'

'No, I never did that. I didn't say anything to Scott. It was his decision. But none of us could possibly know what was going to happen. What's more, we don't even know that it came here through Scott.'

'*I* know! *I* don't have any doubt. And that's my last word, Linda. You're not to bring up his name ever again. He's gone, and good riddance.' He stood up. 'I'm going to bed.'

When he had gone, Linda switched off the television and simply sat staring into space. She felt helpless, torn in two by the gulf that had opened between the two men in her life, leaving a part of her on each side, understanding yet able to do nothing to mend things.

Eight

On Monday afternoon, Rosalind arranged to meet John Parker at the manse. She didn't tell him it was her day off. 'You really must stop doing this, Rosie,' Alastair had said at breakfast, when she told him what she planned. 'You're not superhuman. You need days off like everyone else.'

'Ah, but I've had a very easy weekend,' she had pointed out, though she knew he was not convinced.

The minister was enthusiastic about Rosalind's suggestions for meeting the emergency in the dale, but had to admit that he lacked the computer skills necessary to set up live worship on the Internet. 'My kids are keen on computers, but they're a bit young to have that much expertise,' he said.

'I could try Josh,' Rosalind told him, 'but he's very difficult to pin down during term time, and if I do get him he's in a hurry to be somewhere else. He'll be back here for Easter, I think, but that's leaving it rather late.'

'Certainly, if we could get something up and running by Holy Week, that would be ideal.' That gave them just under two weeks.

'There is Sally Oldfield. I could have a word with her.' They agreed on that, and then moved on to the matter of the helpline. 'I know the NFU has a helpline,' Rosalind said. 'And so does MAFF, but they deal with specific practical enquiries, not emotional and personal problems, still less spiritual ones; they're not there to *listen*.' John Parker agreed to make the necessary enquiries from the telephone companies, after which, so long as the project

83

seemed feasible, they would arrange a meeting with the other clergy in the dale to discuss the details.

Rosalind went straight from the manse to Rose Cottage. By now it was early evening, and it was Lisa who opened the door to her. She ran upstairs to find Sally and while Rosalind waited a young man put his head round the door that led from the kitchen. Rosalind knew his face but could not place him; he clearly knew her too, for he said 'Hi!' and then retreated, as if a little embarrassed. Lisa soon returned with Sally close behind. The girl immediately left them together in the residents' lounge while she went into the kitchen.

'Do you know who the boy in the kitchen is?' Rosalind asked. 'I know we've met, and I ought to know, but I can't place him.'

'It's Scott Emerson, from Middle Byers.'

'Oh, so he and Lisa are an item, are they?'

'I'm not sure. I think so. But that's not why he's here. His father turfed him out.'

'Dear me! What's he done?'

'I think it's because he was working for Armstrongs' when Middle Byers got hit by foot-and-mouth – you know, the animal haulage place in Moor Lane. I gather Dave Emerson blamed Scott for bringing it on to the farm. I doubt if it was as simple as that, but I suppose we all look for someone to blame at times like this. He hadn't wanted Scott working there anyway, which made it worse.'

'Poor lad! It must be terrible for them all, even for his father. Dave Emerson didn't strike me as the sort of man to bear grudges.'

'This disease brings out all sorts of horrible things in people. It makes you feel so helpless.'

Rosalind glanced at her companion's haunted face and abruptly changed the subject. 'And I'm sure you don't want to be reminded of it every minute of the day. I'll tell you why I'm here.' She outlined the live worship project to Sally, who listened with great care, asked a number of questions, and then considered the matter for a moment or two.

84

'It's not that easy,' she said. 'You could just use a webcam – you know, one of those little things you put on the top of the computer. But it would be pretty amateurish stuff, and it wouldn't work for a whole service with a congregation. One individual talking – yes, that would be OK, but that's hardly worship. You could get the sermon that way, I suppose.'

'Isn't there some sort of proper camcorder thing you can link to a computer – the sort of thing they use at weddings and christenings these days?'

'For that to work you need a broadband link.' Sally could see that the reference meant absolutely nothing to Rosalind. She struggled to give a simplified explanation. 'It makes it possible to have much quicker, more complicated Internet connections. In urban areas no business would consider being without it. But it's not cheap – you have to lay a special cable – and BT won't lay it on unless they can be sure of widespread uptake, which of course you're not going to get in remote rural areas.'

'We're not that remote!'

'We are as far as they're concerned.'

'But surely rural businesses depend on efficient computer links even more than urban ones?'

'Tell that to BT.'

'Then why don't the local authorities help?'

'In our case, because it costs money and they're a Labour authority with few votes out here. Or that's how it looks.'

Rosalind considered the matter. 'So, at the very least, the live worship idea's a non-starter? Except for sermons, and I can't think someone just standing there preaching's going to go down too well on the whole.'

'I think so. Sorry.'

'A pity. But it does seem to me that someone ought to be putting on pressure to get this broadband connection. Presumably there has been some approach made?'

'Oh, a few people here and there, yes, certainly. We tried ourselves, because it would have helped in publicizing and selling our produce. But we couldn't afford to pay for the link up front, so we all get the same answer. Not viable.

Elaine Robson here is another one who'd benefit from broadband – I've been giving her a hand with setting up a website, but you can only do so much without the extra speed.'

'Then why don't we all get together? This crisis under-lines the need even more. We need publicity, don't we?'

'Maybe this isn't the moment, with foot-and-mouth making all the headlines. Then there'll be the election, I suppose . . .'

'Just the right moment for a bit of pressure on our MP, don't you think?'

Sally laughed. 'I'm with you on that.'

'Will you help me with a letter? If we send it off soon, then once the election meetings start we can begin increasing the pressure, and he'll be forewarned.'

'Good idea,' said Sally. 'We should get as many signa-tures as possible. Normally that would be easy, but we're going to have to keep it here in the village. A pity, because farmers would benefit as much as anyone. But I'm happy to tout for signatures. It'll give me something to do. Would you like me to draft the letter?'

'That would be great. Something to stir Ted Desmond's conscience. Now, that's enough politics. How are you? And how's Ben?'

Sally's face darkened. 'Oh, I'm fine, everything's going well with the baby. But Ben – well, he's getting very low. I wanted to go home, but he says no. They haven't finished all the disinfection yet and he doesn't want me around while that's going on. And of course he'll be in quarantine for a while yet.'

'Then they did find foot-and-mouth in your animals after all?' That, Rosalind thought, would be a sort of relief, to know there was a point to the destruction of their animals.

'We haven't got the results back yet. We're sure they'll be negative. But you still have to go through the quarantine whatever.'

No relief then. 'How soon will you be able to restock?'

'Oh, not for months yet – but to be honest I don't think

we will. We've more or less decided that once this is all over, we'll put the house on the market and get back to city life.'

Rosalind felt genuinely dismayed. 'Oh, I'm sorry! But don't you think country life will be better for your baby?'

'What, and risk having to go through all this again? Oh no, we've had enough. I certainly have.' She smiled faintly. 'Computer viruses I can cope with – but this one, seeing all our animals slaughtered . . . No, I couldn't face that again. I can't imagine ever having peace of mind if we were to stay here.' Then she added, 'But while we are here, I'm happy to do what I can to make life easier for those who have the guts to stay. I'll give you a ring when I've done that letter so you can give it the once-over and make any suggestions for improvement.'

Rosalind went home in a thoughtful mood. So much for her grand ideas! But here then was another way in which country people felt discriminated against – to be deprived of a tool that would have made such a huge difference to their working lives. Then there were the personal agonies that this current epidemic had brought about – Sally's separation from Ben; Ben's depression; the rift between father and son at Middle Byers. Rosalind had met Linda Emerson in the village one day and gathered she was back at work, but she had said nothing of what had happened. Perhaps she had felt it would be disloyal to Dave, but she must be carrying a terrible burden of misery, on top of all the usual ones brought by foot-and-mouth disease.

Once back in her study, Rosalind offered prayers for them all, asking that if there was any way in which she could help to heal the rift, she might be shown what it was. Then she telephoned John Parker, to let him know Sally's view about the possibility of live services on the Internet. He in turn told her he'd found that a helpline could be set up within twenty-four hours of any request they made; so they arranged an early date for a meeting with the area dean, the Baptist minister and the Catholic priest to discuss the details.

'We really need volunteers with some sort of counselling skills – experience with the Samaritans, or something
on those lines,' Father Preston advised when they were
together. 'I know you have a formal qualification, Rosalind,
and most of us, in the course of our ministries, have amassed
a good deal of informal experience. But we must be prepared
to vet any volunteers who come forward. A tricky one, since
we don't want to put people off.'

'You're right, though,' Rosalind agreed. 'I think every
church has the sort of people who are eager to help but
blunder in with hobnailed boots. We need listeners, not
advisers.'

They took some time to decide on the wording of an
appeal to their respective congregations, and then agreed to
set up the helpline with themselves and any other qualified
people manning the line until a full quota of volunteers
was available. They approached the Samaritans for advice
and arranged a few training sessions for any volunteers
with little experience but obvious gifts. They also succeeded in enlisting the help of a part-time worker with
the Citizens' Advice Bureau, who could give advice on
further information available. They advertised the service
on their respective websites, through the local Farmers'
Union representatives, and by means of leaflets sent out
through the post to the remote boxes set at farm gateways.

Rosalind also took it upon herself to contact people to
find out what they wanted from a helpline, and what else
might help them at this time. It was an excuse to phone
Middle Byers, where Dave Emerson answered the phone.
Rosalind wondered whether to ask to speak to Linda instead,
but then told herself this might be God's way of offering her
the opportunity she had prayed for, a means of intervening
for good in the breach between father and son.

'Would you have a moment to tell me what you think
about a scheme we're about to put in place?' she began
cautiously.

'What would that be then?' He sounded wary, suspicious.

'It's a helpline, for anyone who's wanting help or advice during the foot-and-mouth outbreak, but especially for farmers.'

'The union's already got one.'

'I know. But this would be set up by the churches in Meadhope, though it wouldn't just be for church people. We're hoping to make it available twenty-four hours a day, either just to listen, or to refer people on to other bodies that can answer any questions they might have. Obviously, the union can help with a lot of practical things, but not everything.'

'Sounds OK, I suppose. But I'm not a great one for all this counselling stuff. Get on with living, that's what I believe.'

'But you think some people might find it helpful?'

'Why yes, some might.'

'Then you haven't any suggestions as to the kind of information we could offer?'

'Not that comes to mind, no.'

'Would you let me know if you think of anything?' She heard him agree, then she paused a moment before saying, 'I saw your son the other day, at Rose Cottage.'

'I've no son,' said Dave, and she heard the click as he put the receiver down.

'That went well!' she thought unhappily. She'd handled it clumsily – blundered in with hobnailed boots, in fact. Now, without doubt, he would think she had phoned only to talk about Scott; which in a way was true.

Later that afternoon, she was surprised to receive a call from Linda. 'Dave was telling me about your call,' she said. 'I think it's a great idea. There are a lot of people need someone to talk to in confidence, even if they're not desperate enough for the Samaritans. Even when it comes to practical things, the union doesn't cover everything.'

'I don't suppose we'll cover everything either.'

'So long as you don't put anything off limits, that'll be good.' There was a little silence, during which Rosalind wondered whether she should bring up the subject of Scott.

Then Linda said, 'Dave thought you were phoning up about Scott. He thought I'd put you up to it.'

'Oh, I'm so sorry – I never meant . . .' So she'd made a bad situation worse!

'No – no, I'm glad you phoned. At least you tried. I keep trying myself, but I get nowhere. He just won't listen. I had thought of phoning you about it anyway. He's out mending a wall, so I called you back. I just don't know what to do for the best.'

'Do you think he'll come round, in time?'

'I tell myself he will. But he shows no signs of it. He's still talking about selling up, as soon as the epidemic's over.'

'But his family's been there for generations!'

'I know. You see how bad it is.'

First the Oldfields, now the Emersons – what would the dale be like when all this was over? A lovely wasteland, with land too marginal to be attractive to the businessmen to whom farming was simply another investment opportunity? An empty landscape taken over by scrub and weeds, with farmhouses left derelict because they were too remote, too cut off from any easy means of communication with the outside world to be occupied by any but the very rich? It was a grim vision, made the more terrible because of the human pain that threatened to bring it about. And what could she do to make things better? What comfort could she offer this divided family? How could she help them to find healing?

'Would you like me to try and talk to Dave again? Or would there be any point in talking to Scott?'

'Scott wants to make it up. He's really depressed about it. He's lost his job too – he's looking for other work, but there's nothing going; not in the dale anyway. If he moves away, that's like admitting defeat. As for Dave – well, I don't suppose he'd talk to you anyway.'

Rosalind felt useless, inadequate. She knew all things were possible with God, but that did not mean she was the agent He would use in every circumstance, however much she might wish it were so. For now, she could only resort to the usual phrases, which sounded like banalities, though they were not. 'I'm sure things will get better, in time. You know you're all in my prayers. Meanwhile, if I think of anything, I'll be in touch. And you know where I am if you want to talk, any time.'

Within days, the helpline was set up, the volunteers taking turns to wait by the phone in a small, dark room at the back of the church hall, chosen because it was compact and relatively soundproof. Rosalind took her first turn of duty on the following Monday – she had not felt it right to take time from her normal parish duties for such an activity, so gave up an afternoon and evening of her day off. She had brought work with her to do – two weighty theological books and the minutes of the last meeting of the Parochial Church Council, to help her prepare the agenda for the next one in two weeks' time. For the first hour and a half of her session she had ample opportunity to concentrate on repairs to the church roof, the rising diocesan quota, plans for the church summer fair – which might have to be cancelled altogether, in view of the continuing foot-and-mouth epidemic – and other parish minutiae.

The phone shrilling suddenly into the silence made her jump. A momentary panic sent her books slithering to the floor as she clutched at the receiver. She grabbed the piece of paper with the introductory words written on it and read as calmly as she could. 'Dale helpline. How can I help you?' The words sounded silly and artificial, like those of a McDonald's assistant, but it was what they had agreed on. As she spoke, Rosalind braced herself for whatever anguish might be on the other end of the line.

'I'm looking for someone to pop in and see my mam once a week. She doesn't get out, and now I can't.'

With a sigh of relief, Rosalind reached for her pad and wrote down the old lady's name and address. She then found out a little more about her – that she'd never been a regular churchgoer, but had been brought up a Catholic; that she liked a tipple now and then, a nip of whisky at bedtime; that she had meals on wheels, but didn't like them much;

91

that she complained constantly about the care workers who came in three times a week to do her ironing and cleaning; that neighbours did her shopping, but few stayed to talk to her, which was why she depended on her son's visits. She noted these points, but did not add what she read between the lines – that the old lady was cantankerous and difficult. Then she reassured the caller that his mother would be visited and heard the relief and satisfaction in his voice. Not a difficult problem then, but one that meant a good deal to the dutiful son. This was one for Father Preston, who could call on one of his flock to visit; failing that, she herself would find somebody suitable. She wondered if Linda Emerson knew the old lady, and if it would be a breach of confidence to ask her.

The phone rang again, twice in swift succession. The first caller was an angry farmer who had just heard that his now-dead animals had tested negative for foot-and-mouth, wanting to sound off about the firebreak cull, about his rage at seeing healthy animals killed unnecessarily. Rosalind listened, which was all that seemed to be required of her; at least until he demanded, 'You there, you can get out and see people – tell them what's happening, see if you can change things!' She was about to say that this was how the authorities felt they could best end the outbreak; then she thought better of it. Presumably the man on the line knew that already, which was why he felt so helpless. In the end she promised to put his views to the appropriate people, though she hadn't much idea who they would be. This was perhaps something to bring to the next meeting of the helpline volunteers.

By now, the Meadhope Choral Society had moved into the hall at the further end of the building. The sound of chatter, interspersed with the notes of the piano, reached her in occasional bursts. Alastair would be there, she thought, and found comfort in the knowledge. Then the singing began, in full-throated bursts, broken off at irregular inter-vals to be followed by some repeated passage or other, before the flow was resumed. The familiar choruses of

Stainer's *Crucifixion*, distant but unmistakable, succeeded one another, companions to her vigil. It might not be her favourite work, but there was something safe and reassuring about its familiarity, the memories evoked from her childhood; the sense that there were continuities, even in this world where suddenly all the old ways seemed to have no place.

After about two hours the singing came to an end, and she heard the sounds of people departing, in twos and threes, chatting as they went, calling goodnight. Alastair would now be back at the rectory, watching the news before going to bed – she had told him not to wait up. By now it was fully dark, and near the end of her session. She began to gather her books and papers together, ready to hand over to her replacement. And then the phone rang suddenly, startling her. She drew a deep breath to steady herself after the surprise of it, and lifted the receiver. She spoke the usual words, trying to inject some note of sincerity into them, and waited. There was silence, broken only by a few gasping breaths – someone in real anguish? Or a heavy breather, seeking a new audience? 'Hello,' she coaxed. 'My name's Rosalind. I'm listening.'

'Aye, well . . .' Anguish – she recognized that now. The two words sounded harsh, croaking, more like a groan than ordinary speech.

She waited.

'They've gone, the lot of them. Do you know what it's like? Thirty-five years of work, gone. Nowt left. Just . . . nowt. Silence.' He was, she thought now, a little drunk, perhaps very drunk, but she knew this was a result of his pain, not the cause of it. 'You, listen!' There was a pause. The sound of the breathing grew fainter. After a second or two she realized what was happening – he was holding the handset out, away from his ear, so that she could hear the silence that surrounded him. Then he was back. 'See? Nowt. Not a sound.' She thought then that he was actually sobbing, though the sounds were harsh and strange, as if such a response was wholly alien to him. 'There's a stink, though.

No one's been to bury them. Not a soul. Four days since they shot them. Just a stink. Do you know what that's like?'

She paused before answering, since some sort of answer seemed to be expected. She could hardly say yes – she could only guess what it was like, what he must be feeling, and he wouldn't have believed her anyway, but she knew she must get the words right. 'I don't know,' she said. 'But it shouldn't happen like that.'

'You're dead right it shouldn't. Dead right.'

'Have you phoned the Ministry? Do they know what's happening?'

The voice changed to bitter mimicry. '"Why yes, Mr Bell, we're aware of the problem. We're doing our best. We'll be along as soon as ever we can." Problem! That's all it is to them. A little problem, which they can't even be buggered to solve!'

Rosalind registered the name: Mr Bell – was that Colin Bell, alone at isolated High Intake farm? Bell was a common enough name in this area, but she thought it was likely all the same. She knew his land was vulnerable, in the very heart of the local outbreak. 'Would you like me to speak to them? Do you think that might help?'

'I doubt it. You can try if you want to. You know what? I reckon this is what Blair and his lot want. Wreck farming, kill off all the little farms. Put all the money in the pockets of the big agribusiness barons.' He stumbled over the long word. 'Efficient farming – that's what they call it. Turn the bits they can't farm like that into theme parks.'

'I don't suppose the government wanted this outbreak any more than you did.'

'Then why wipe out all those animals, all of them? Healthy animals. Just gone.' He was sobbing again.

'I'll phone the Ministry people,' she assured him. 'They know we're keeping an eye on what they're doing. If that doesn't shift them, then I'll get on to the MP and the papers. At least then you should soon get your farm cleared and be able to start again. This epidemic has to end one day.'

'It'll be too late for me,' the man said. There was an

94

abrupt click and the dialling tone buzzed into the sudden silence.

Anxious, Rosalind immediately rang the number back, but she heard it ringing and ringing endlessly, unanswered. She tried two or three times, with the same result.

Then she telephoned the number they had been given for the Ministry veterinary service and expressed her outrage at what she had been told. She was assured the disposal of Mr Bell's animals was next on the list, possibly tomorrow afternoon. They were doing the best they could in a very difficult situation. 'That doesn't seem to me good enough,' she replied crisply, and rang off. She tried the farm a couple more times, hoping that this near-promise might be enough to raise the farmer a little from his despair, but there was still no answer. Then Keith Grey, one of Meadhope's churchwardens, a sensitive man who had been through difficult times himself, arrived to relieve her. She told him something of the call she'd taken and what she'd done about it – enough for him to know the background if the man should ring again.

'I'll keep trying to get in touch again if you think it's a good idea,' he offered. 'Or do you think he'll mind knowing you've spoken to me about him?'

'I don't know. I suppose he might even prefer to speak to a man. Some do.'

She made her way home, feeling drained. It was raining and cold, but the fresh air was consoling. Even more consoling was to find Alastair still up, coming to welcome her with a hug. 'Tough day?' he asked, looking into her face.

'Very tough. Sometimes I feel so inadequate.'

'You're not. Believe me, you're not. It's the people who think they have all the solutions who are inadequate. Anyway, where's the person who's always telling me God will make up the shortfall?'

She smiled. 'Here in your arms. Thanks, love. Let's go to bed.'

'Oh, by the way,' he said as they went upstairs, 'Sophie rang. The worst's happened, as far as she's concerned.

They've called her in to help with the Cumbrian outbreak.'

So their own family was touched too, ensnared in this
horrible thing. Rosalind shivered. 'Poor Sophie. I'll give
her a ring tomorrow.'

Nine

There was something soothing to Rosalind about the round of hospital visits she made on Tuesday morning. This was ordinary parish work, bringing the church's ministry to the old and the ill, in a way that she knew gave comfort, in a way that was expected of her – face to face in simple human contact. By the time she drove home again for a hastily snatched lunch, she felt that the strains of yesterday were behind her, over and done with. She had a niggle of anxiety about Sophie, of course, but she tried to put that aside until she was forced to face it, until she spoke to Sophie next. For now, for this afternoon, her concern was with the forthcoming services for Holy Week, which she wanted to have finalized before Josh came home for the Easter vacation the very next day. A few days before, she had talked to Daphne Wynyard about the services that would normally have taken place at Ashburn, and agreed that they should be cancelled, apart from a single celebration of holy communion on Palm Sunday and then again on Easter Day. Now she needed to finalize the arrangements with Daphne, in case there were any new developments to take into account.

Back to foot-and-mouth, Rosalind thought, drawing a deep breath as she dialled the number for Ashburn Hall. 'How are things with you?' she asked when Daphne answered. By now, there were so many cases of foot-and-mouth, once you included the farms caught in the contiguous cull, that the local paper had stopped listing every case, unless it had some especially newsworthy significance, so Rosalind found it hard to keep track of which of her parishioners had been hit.

'We've lost our beasts, if that's what you mean,' said Daphne baldly. 'Contiguous cull. No trace of disease – tests came back negative. But too late by then, of course.' She paused, giving Rosalind a clear sense that there was about to be some sort of explosion. It came a moment later. 'Not to mince words –' Did she ever? Rosalind asked herself '– I'm furious. Hopping mad, spitting with rage. I can't believe there could be such incompetence, such complete and utter bloody incompetence.'

'You don't subscribe to this conspiracy theory I've been hearing then? That if they didn't exactly start the epidemic, the government at least saw its chance to make use of it to destroy so-called uneconomic farms?'

'Tosh! But not *utter* tosh. The long and short of it is, Blair and his lot have no more idea about country life than does your average East End barrow boy. And they care less, so long as it doesn't cause them inconvenience. All that about taking personal charge – that was only because he could see that all those television pictures of burning carcasses were losing him votes. Well, I can tell you, once all this is behind us, he's going to find we cause him one hell of a lot more inconvenience. By the time we've finished with him he'll understand about country life for sure. We've been pushed around and ignored long enough.'

Rosalind, who knew that much of Daphne's anger was still directed at the anti-hunting faction within the Labour party, found it hard to be as sympathetic as she knew she ought to be. She thought it was as well she had no need to say much, for Daphne was doing all the talking. Later, after she rang off, the other woman's rage seemed to echo in her head.

Which, Rosalind thought, was the emotion emerging most strongly from the present crisis: rage, a truly bitter rage, fed by a sense of being consistently ignored and misunderstood. The mood, if not the reasons for it, had something familiar about it, which Rosalind could not quite place, though it echoed through her, chiming against some unremembered past experience. She considered the matter as she went to church for evensong, and there, alone in the silent building, as she murmured the words of the Magnificat, it suddenly came back to her. There *had* been another occasion when she had carried bitterness like this into the day's worship, another occasion when the powerful, familiar phrases had taken on a new significance. 'He has put down the mighty from their thrones: and has lifted up the lowly. He has filled the hungry with good things: and the rich he has sent away empty.'

At Coldwell she had come to evensong one evening, full of the anger and bitterness that had filled the voice of an unemployed miner she had visited that afternoon – a man in his early forties who had not worked since the Coldwell pit had closed following the disastrous strike of 1984. He had spoken, as so many did in those days, about how under the years of Thatcher government he felt disenfranchised, as if there was no one to speak for him and his kind. Rosalind, who had seen how the community in which she then lived had crumbled and decayed; how, in the worst cases, many places became lawless deserts, had understood what he meant, and in those words of the Magnificat had seen both a comment on their plight and a message of hope.

Now she understood something of what Daphne felt – and Colin Bell too, as he'd poured his despair down the line to her last night. Just as the miners and the other communities who depended on the old industries had felt that they had no voice, no one to speak for them during the years of Conservative government, so now the farmers, seeing their livelihoods destroyed, felt much the same way. And there was a certain truth in that, Rosalind acknowledged, for even if it was incompetence rather than malice that dictated the way the outbreak was being handled, it was certain enough that none of the decision-makers were looking at the matter through the eyes of the small hill farmers of this lovely valley. Their hardship might be less obvious to the outsider than that of the miners, for they lived in beautiful houses with breathtaking views, and they were compensated for their losses, after a fashion, and subsidized as the miners had never been. But their sense of abandonment, of hopelessness was no less real for all that. To Daphne, hunting might be a significant part of the quarrel with those in power, but for most farmers it went much wider than that, to their very reason for living and working. And the farmers lacked the one thing the miners had – a close-knit community, gathered in one place, where for good or ill they could find support in adversity. Of its very nature, farming was an isolating business, where despair was always shivering on the horizon, waiting for a bad harvest, a depressed market.

This evening, when she reached the intercessions at the end of the service, Rosalind prayed for the suffering of the community in which she lived, the real and terrible suffering, and the sense of abandonment that made it all so much harder to bear.

She returned to the rectory after evensong to find the phone ringing. 'It's Barry Preston here.' Sergeant Preston was the police officer responsible for liaison between the local police station and the dale; he lived in Meadhope. 'Bad news, I'm afraid. Colin Bell's been found dead up at High Intake. Shot himself, they think. They found him this afternoon when they turned up to clear the carcasses of his animals. There'll have to be a post-mortem, of course, but there's no family anyone knows of, and he never had many vistors. Thought you'd be as good a person as any to let know. Someone said they thought you'd visited there recently.'

Not just that, but she had spoken to him last night. Faltering, her heart thudding, she told the sergeant what had happened. When the call ended, Rosalind sat on at her desk, gazing at nothing in particular, while the darkness deepened about her.

Alastair found her like this when he came home half an hour later. He pushed open the study door and put his head round. 'Hi!' Then he pushed the door wider and came in. 'Rosie?' He bent over the desk and switched on the reading lamp. 'What's amiss, love?'

She raised haunted eyes to his face. 'Colin Bell – he's shot

100

himself.' She saw that the name meant nothing to Alastair. 'Farmer, up at High Intake, beyond where the Oldfields live. He lives – *lived* – by himself. He was caught in the firebreak cull last week.'

Alastair came round the desk and pulled her into his arms. 'Rosie, darling! You mustn't let these things get to you like this.' He was puzzled. 'It's terrible, I know—'

'Alastair, I was almost certainly the last person to speak to him. He called the helpline last night, just before I left. I could tell he was distraught, but I didn't know what to say to help. I tried, God knows I tried. But it was too much for me and now this has happened. I should have found something – anything – to say, to stop him going as far as this!'

He stroked her hair. 'Rosie, darling, even you're not superhuman. You know yourself, sometimes there are people who are quite simply beyond your help, beyond any help.'

'Not beyond *any* help – I have to believe that's never true. But now! Besides, of course I'm not superhuman, but with God's help anything should be possible, so long as we allow it – so long as *I* allow it.'

Alastair struggled to find the right words to help her – as perhaps she had struggled to help Colin Bell, though in this case he knew it was not a fight for life, but part of something simpler, yet just as profound – the ordinary, everyday search for explanation, for truth, in which Rosalind had been engaged for most of her life. To a limited extent he understood that search and shared in it, as most human beings did, but he knew that for his wife it was a part of her as it had never been for him – the heart and centre, the focal point of her daily life. Now he sensed that a great deal was going on within Rosalind's thoughts that he could only glimpse, and for which she alone had to find an answer. He could not travel on that journey with her. He could only offer support and consolation, gentle words and loving arms, and hope that was enough to take the edge from her pain as she travelled further on her way.

After a time, he asked gently, 'Will they be wanting you at the inquest?'

101

'The police think so. I have to go and give them a statement, too.'

He rubbed her shoulders, kissed her again, then said, 'I'll get supper.'

'There's a casserole I took out of the freezer this morning.'

'Then I'll go and heat it up. Ready in ten minutes or so.'

'Give me a little while – half an hour. If you can bear to wait so long?'

'Of course.' One more kiss on her forehead and he left her.

Rosalind spent the half hour in silent prayer, wrestling with her sense of inadequacy, with her knowledge of the farmer's solitary, desperate end. She could only offer that despair to God, trusting in His mercy to put it all right, to give peace to the lonely man, to forgive her inadequacy, to forgive all who had failed him. Then she prayed for all those still living who were struggling in solitude against despair and hopelessness; prayed that they might find help and consolation before it was too late.

By the time she joined Alastair in the kitchen she felt calmer, ready to accept her failure and put it aside. 'You need a talk with your father,' he suggested.

After supper, she took up his suggestion and dialled her parents' number. Her mother listened to her for a short time, then handed her over to her father. William Percival somehow found parallels within his own ministry, where he too had often been faced with a sense of inadequacy, and had also learned to come to terms with it and move on.

'I don't know what I'd do without you!' Rosalind told him at the end of their conversation. In her early days as a priest she had often kept from him the things that troubled her, being afraid to burden him with them, or perhaps, more truly, being afraid to reveal her own failings to parents who were so proud of her. Now she'd realized that to William Percival, who had walked a very similar path throughout his life, it was not a burden but a joy to be able to help her, if only by listening; and there was sufficient equality in their relationship for her to accept that help.

The following Sunday was Palm Sunday, the day of the first concert given by the new Meadhope Choral Society, the performance of Stainer's *Crucifixion*. Somehow the choice of music, the time, the place, had all seemed to offer something that was much needed, and nearly a hundred people walked or drove to the church through the rain to hear the music, many of them people who had no usual connection with the place. Rosalind found herself unexpectedly moved by the performance, which was sung with real fervour. Its message of redemption and boundless love seemed tonight to be stripped of its Victorian sentimentality, to become precisely what the moment needed. At the end, there came that moment of silence in the congregation, which was the surest indication that a performance had struck home. One or two people, pausing in the doorway to speak to Rosalind afterwards, had visible tears in their eyes as they spoke of what the performance had meant to them. One of those was Joan Sheffield, from the farm adjacent to the Oldfields that had so recently suffered the loss of all its stock. 'Today's the first day I've left the farm since we were hit,' she said. 'I've heard that piece so many times, but tonight it meant more than it's ever done before. I'm so glad I came.' She held Rosalind's hands in hers. 'This has reminded me that whatever happens, whatever we have to suffer, we're not alone.'

As a further tribute to the singing, the collection plates laid on tables either side of the door were full to overflowing by the time the bulk of the audience had gone. Most of the choir members lingered, to enjoy refreshments provided by the church ladies. Rosalind left Alastair to the cluster of congratulatory singers who thronged about him, and went to help the stalwarts who were stripping the church of all its ornaments, in preparation for Holy Week.

Later, they walked back to the rectory alone together – Josh, home for Easter, had declined to come with them this evening. Rosalind said, 'I take back all I said about *Crucifixion*. I was truly moved by it, and I certainly wasn't the only one. You've done wonders to produce such a fine performance after so short a time.'

'To be honest, as I said, it took very little work, as most people knew it already. As you so wisely pointed out, it's an old warhorse of a piece. But in the right place at the right time, it can work superbly.'

'As it did. It spoke to our condition, I suppose.' She slid her arm through his, huddling under the umbrella he held over both their heads. 'So, what next?'

'I don't know. I'd like to do something more ambitious. Perhaps we should just start practising something really challenging to perform at Christmas, or even next year. Or I might try out a few excerpts from larger works and see how we get on and what might suit us. After all, the choir's got to enjoy any work we do, so they ought to have a say in it.'

'So long as you have the last word,' Rosalind pointed out with a grin.

'Precisely. And a definitive veto. To be honest, I don't know for certain yet quite what they're capable of singing. It's no good choosing something that's beyond us. But I would like something that stretches us a bit. Anyway, we'll see. For the moment we're taking a break until the autumn. Hopefully by then this horrible thing will be over.'

'Please God!' said Rosalind fervently.

Ten

They had reached the solemnity of Holy Week, with its daily evening meditations on the Passion, to which a small group of Rosalind's most faithful parishioners came. It was always the most intense period for any priest, this time leading up to the great festival of Easter. Even in normal times it would have been exhausting, but now, in the midst of the ravages of foot-and-mouth, it not only felt more solemn, but there were more than the usual number of calls on her time. She did not feel able to refuse to take her place in the helpline rota, though she had to adjust her shift to fit in with the services. So on the Monday she took her place early in the day, immediately after mattins, taking a sandwich with her for lunch. She absorbed three long unhappy calls in the course of the next few hours, from farmers or their wives who simply wanted someone to listen, calls full of the usual bitterness and anger and grief.

The last caller, a woman who had once been a reasonably regular attender at church, knew who Rosalind was at once – had even perhaps expected her to answer – for she asked, 'Where's God in all this, that's what I want to know?'

'Alongside you all, with arms outstretched in love,' Rosalind answered promptly. 'Isn't that the message of this Holy Week? That God shared our human suffering?'

'What use is that if it doesn't make things better? No, rector, even if I could, I wouldn't be in church this week. It's not just Tony Blair and his lot who've betrayed us, it's God too. If he exists at all. I'm sorry if that shocks you, but there it is.'

Rosalind tried to find the right words to counter the

woman's bitter argument, but knew afterwards that she had failed, though she held on to a faint hope that, in time, something she had said might be used to revive the woman's faith. But she knew too that, as Good Friday approached, there would be many of her parishioners to whom the death of a charismatic Jewish preacher two thousand years ago was nothing against their own, only too present suffering. She had even heard it said, by someone interviewed on the radio, that the countryside was being crucified.

Later, she fitted in a visit to a bereaved family – the funeral was to take place on Wednesday – and then was home in time for a snatched evening meal prepared by Alastair, who was on holiday this week. 'Josh has taken himself off to Durham for the day,' he told her. 'Meeting . . . oh, one of the lads from Coldwell, I think.' He brought cauliflower cheese and baked potatoes to the table, giving his wife an intent look before he began to transfer the food to their plates. 'You look tired, Rosie, and it's only the start of Holy Week. And what's happened to our usual post-Easter holiday? Have I missed out on the plans?'

'You know I couldn't go away so soon after arriving here – that would be true even in normal times. And these aren't normal times.' She began to eat. 'Did you manage to get your mother?' Very often, Alastair's mother came from her Edinburgh home to spend Easter with them, but they had still not heard whether she planned to do the same this year.

'I did, and she's not coming.' He grinned. 'Don't look so relieved! She decided that it would be irresponsible of her to come to a plague-ridden area and risk spreading disease.'

'Well, I suppose she has to consider the farmers of Morningside,' observed Rosalind with heavy irony; Alastair's mother lived in a select residential area. 'Or is she afraid she might catch it?'

'Probably,' said Alastair; his mother was one of those people who go in terror of germs. 'Anyway, we can relax for the moment. I'll have to get to see her some time, but there's no hurry.'

Rosalind glanced at the clock. 'There is for me! Six

thirty already – I must dash.' She gulped down a final mouthful, kissed Alastair and raced upstairs to tidy herself before running across the churchyard for the seven o'clock service.

As she returned to the house an hour later, she heard the phone ringing. She felt her heart thud; since the helpline had been set up the sound of a phone had an ominous sound. 'I'll get it!' she called to Alastair, who she could hear was watching television in the sitting room. She went into the study and picked up the handset, assuming the warm, neutral tones with which she always answered the rectory phone. 'Meadhope rectory; Rosalind Maclaren speaking.'

Before she reached the end of her sentence, she heard the familiar voice at the other end. 'Mum? It's me.'

'Sophie!' Relief swept over her. 'How good to hear you! How are things?'

But it was not good – already something in Sophie's tone had warned her of that. There was a little pause before her daughter said, 'I wish I could come home!'

'You can, darling. You know you're always welcome!' Rosalind was puzzled, because she could tell from Sophie's tone that her daughter was expressing a wish for something she knew could only be a dream, unrealizable.

'I can't. I can't go anywhere. Mum, you know they called me in to help with the epidemic? I've spent two days killing sheep – lambs, mostly. Then I'm quarantined. I can't get it out of my head, any of it. Mum, it's horrendous, awful – I can't begin to tell you . . .'

Rosalind was swept by a sense of helpless maternity. All she wanted to do now was gather her daughter into her arms, to kiss away all her troubles, as she would have done when she was a little girl, waking at midnight from a nightmare. But this nightmare was real and her daughter was miles away from her, cut off from any consolation from those she loved; and she was also an adult, who had to find her own path through the horror that had engulfed her. 'Are there people you work with who can help you?'

'No one, Mum, no one at all. All day I'm out killing

animals, then at night I come back to this place and I have to stay here.'

'Where are you? Where's "this place"?'

'It's a holiday cottage on the first farm I had to go to. No one's renting it, of course. So MAFF requisitions them to accommodate us. It's not bad, I suppose. Two bedrooms, nice views, a bit damp, especially in this weather. But I don't want to look out on empty fields when I know what they mean – *all* they mean. And there's no one to share it with me – I suppose because I'm the only woman working round here and they didn't think it would be right to put me up with a man. Oh Mum, what I'd give to be able to come home to you at the end of the day!'

It was, Rosalind thought, a measure of her daughter's anguish that she should not only want her mother to care for her, but also admitted openly to such a weakness. That her headstrong, independent daughter should be brought to this only intensified Rosalind's pain. If she could have dropped everything and gone to Sophie's side she would have done so at once. But of course it was not possible, and she suspected that even if it had been, when it came to the point, Sophie would not really have wanted it.

She tried to take Sophie's mind off the horror of what she was experiencing by talking of ordinary happy things, though it was hard to find enough to talk about when so much of her own daily life was taken up with the repercussions of the very same disease that was causing Sophie such pain. She resorted to talking about Josh, though that did not provide much food for conversation either, since he was very uncommunicative about anything except practical things, like food and how he was to get his washing done. They agreed, like old fogeys, that he drank too much, and speculated about the progress of his social life, and whether or not he was still with the girl whose name he had mentioned, briefly, last Christmas – Sophie thought not. Then Rosalind went to bring Alastair to the phone, and he too talked of harmless, everyday things. By the time Sophie rang off over an hour later, she sounded rather more cheerful, almost herself. Rosalind guessed that it would not last, but a small respite was better than none.

That was the horror of this disease, she thought. It shut everyone up in their own confined space, cut them off from all the normal things that helped them to face what life threw at them; from family, friends, neighbours. Rosalind guessed that even for those who were quarantined on their farms with their families around them, it was hard to find help, for so often they must begin to rub each other up the wrong way, to get on one another's nerves – exactly as had apparently happened to the Emersons at Middle Byers. And here was she – who should be preaching that no one was alone, that God could turn any suffering to good – finding it hard to cope with her daughter's lonely misery.

Alastair put his arm about her. 'She'll be all right, love. She's tough, our Sophie.'

'I know, but this . . . no one should have to go through things like this.'

'A great many people are, one way and another.'

'It gives an added poignancy to Holy Week. We don't need to make any effort to imagine suffering – it's here all around us. Just a little part of the burden of Good Friday.'

'Which ends in Easter,' Alastair reminded her, in words she might herself have used. Then he kissed her.

They heard the front door open and Josh came in; he looked unusually excited, elated even.

'Good day?' Rosalind asked.

'OK,' was all he said, in a tone that belied the offhand reply.

They asked after the friend he had been meeting, but it seemed to take him a moment or two to realize what they were talking about and his reply was brief and uninformative. Since he was clearly unwilling to offer any more information, they told him about his sister's call, and he promised to contact her soon, if only to provide another listener for her troubles. Then he said goodnight and went up to his room, where he lay on his bed going over the night's events in his mind.

Since coming home for the vacation, he had taken to ambling past the front of Rose Cottage at every available opportunity, but to no effect. Now and then he would see someone entering or leaving the place – Elaine, the landlady, perhaps; or a slim, dark youth whom he took to be the girl's brother; or pregnant Sally who was living there, to whom he'd been introduced in church on Sunday. He'd even had an intelligent and interesting conversation with her about the lack of broadband access in the dale. But not once did he so much as catch a glimpse of the girl he had seen on his last visit.

But tonight he'd struck lucky, just when he'd least expected it. He'd enjoyed meeting his old school friend in Durham, but had been disappointed that Dean had another engagement, with a girl, in the evening and couldn't stay for a drink. He'd returned to Meadhope, feeling bored and restless, and by chance had wandered into one of the pubs he had not entered before – largely because it seemed to be the haunt of the middle-aged and elderly – and there he had seen her, talking animatedly to a group of the pub's more typical customers, two women and three men, neatly dressed for a night out – jackets and ties for the men, blouses and skirts for the women.

The place was quite full, so he'd edged his way through the throng until only one other person – a morose-looking man propped on the bar – stood between them. He could hear what she was saying, quite clearly, since she was speaking with evangelical fervour. 'We've got to get it stopped. It was bad enough while all those pyres were burning round here, but up there it could go on for weeks, and no one seems to know what poisons it'll spread around.' She paused long enough for one of the women to agree that she had a point, then went on. 'It could even give off dioxins.' This was clearly her clinching argument – quite rightly, Josh thought, though he had not yet grasped precisely what she was talking about. But it was clear that her audience, unlike him, had no idea what dioxins were; he had also concluded that she was not talking to close friends or acquaintances, that she was not here for any social reason, but that she had come here to gain support for some cause, for which she held a sheaf of leaflets in one hand. He saw that some of the other people in the pub had copies already, and two were even reading them. This was his chance! He pushed his way to her side.

'Excuse me butting in,' he said, 'but I couldn't help overhearing. Dioxins cause cancer, you know, among other things. They're one of the most deadly substances known to man, and very hard to get rid of. That's what the Americans used in Vietnam – Agent Orange. And there was that accident in India years ago, at a chemical plant – you may remember it. I don't, of course, I was too young. But people are still suffering from its effects even now, decades later. That's dioxins for you.' He glanced at the girl, suddenly fearing that she might resent his interference, but she simply looked startled, just for a moment, until she seized the opportunity to make use of what he had said.

'So we have to get it stopped!' she urged. 'The more people make their feelings known, the more likely it is they'll think again. It's happening all over the country, wherever they're setting up these sites.'

'But they've got to do something with all those dead animals,' one of the women pointed out. 'There are too many just to dispose of them on the farms.'

Ah, so that's it! Josh thought. They must be planning one of those large-scale disposal sites for carcasses of culled animals in the area. He reached over and pulled one of the leaflets from her hand, surreptitiously scanning it as she continued her argument.

'Of course they have,' the girl said. 'But it's got to be the right solution, otherwise we could be paying for it for generations – and I don't mean in money, but in the health of ourselves and our children, even our grandchildren. Do you really believe they've thought everything through? It's a panic measure.'

'What would *you* do then? Bury them?'

'They have to be disposed of locally. I'd think rendering would be best. They say there aren't enough places to handle them, but they could find a way, I'm sure. What we don't want is diseased animal carcasses being transported hundreds of miles, spreading disease all the way and then being heaped up to pollute places like this for generations to come.'

By now, Josh had read enough to gather that the proposed site was to be set up beyond the hill-top village of Black Fell, once a thriving hub of the coal and iron industries, now reverted to a largely rural community with high unemployment – like Coldwell, only smaller, with prettier surroundings. It must be only about three miles from Meadhope. He could feel himself becoming enraged, as the girl clearly was, by the very thought of the pollution that was about to threaten this lovely place, and all the people in it.

'Anyway, have one of these,' she was saying now, as she handed leaflets to her listeners. 'We're having a meeting up at Black Fell village hall next Tuesday night, after Easter. The more people come the better.' With a glance at Josh, she moved further on through the crowded pub. Josh, interpreting the glance in his favour, followed her. He was delighted when she turned suddenly and thrust half her sheaf of leaflets into his hands. 'Here, you do some too.' Then she gestured to her left, towards the windows that looked over the street. 'You do that side, I'll do this.'

That was not what he'd had in mind, but Josh bit back his disappointment and set out to proselytize his portion of the bar. He had never done such a thing before and it terrified him, but he dared not refuse for fear of losing the girl's interest altogether. Better to be seen simply as a useful ally in the cause than nothing at all. So, feeling as he supposed a Jehovah's Witness must feel knocking on a front door, he took a deep breath and approached the nearest group of drinkers, forcing what he hoped was a friendly smile.

He managed to dispose of most of his quota of leaflets, but few people were interested in hearing what he had to say. By the time he had covered everyone in his part of the bar, he could see that the girl was still talking animatedly; but then, he told himself, middle-aged men drinking in a pub were much more likely to listen to a pretty girl than a lad like himself, especially one who was only too obviously one of that part of society despised by the respectable: a student.

He went to join her, gesturing to demonstrate his empty hands. She smiled at him, all approval, a smile that shot through his body like a flame. She allowed him to tag along after her as she circulated the rest of the room, and to buy her a drink too – a mere coke, but it was enough to make him believe he might be in with a chance as far as she was concerned. When at last they had tackled everyone and her leaflets too had gone, she said, 'Well, that's it for tonight.'

Before she could say goodbye, he said, 'I'll see you home.' She accepted without comment and they set out along the street.

'You'll be there on Tuesday, won't you?' she asked.

'You bet I will! Can I give you a lift?' He sent up a prayer that a parental car would be available – fate could surely not be so cruel as to deny him that small concession?

'Oh . . . oh, yes, that would be good. Mam was going to run me up there, but I know she'd rather not. Thanks.'

So he had that to look forward to as well. At the door of her house he said, 'See you Tuesday. What time?'

'Six thirty. See you!' She was on the point of walking away when she turned back. 'By the way, I'm Lisa.'

'And I'm Josh.' Well, it was progress, of a sort. Slow, perhaps, but he knew he couldn't rush these things for fear of scaring her off. He was humming to himself as he went on his way. Once back at the rectory, he evaded his parents' questioning as adroitly as he knew how and went upstairs to relive the evening's events in his mind.

Inside Rose Cottage, Scott, who had been slumped in front of the television in the residents' lounge, heard the front door open and close and went to meet Lisa. 'Hi!' she said, but without much warmth.

'Did you get rid of all your leaflets?'

'What's it to you?'

'I care about you. But like I told you, I'm in enough trouble as it is—'

'You mean you can't be arsed to give me a hand. Even though you know what it means to me.'

'You know it's not like that!'

'No I don't.' She walked past him towards the stairs. 'Anyway, I'm going to bed. Goodnight.'

Speechless with frustration and misery, he watched her go. How could he tell her that he simply could not bear to undertake anything that forced him to think of foot-and-mouth disease, that he had simply had enough of the whole subject? In any case, he couldn't get worked up about the disposal site. They had to deal with the carcasses somehow, and he supposed they'd picked a place that would cause minimum upheaval. The only cause he cared about was the most hopeless one of all – to find a way of healing the breach with his father, of being allowed back home. He seemed to have exhausted every possibility. His mother had spoken for him, again and again; he had tried approaching Vicky, waiting for her when she got off the school bus one morning, but she had brushed past him without a word, as if she had not seen him there. Clearly she was taking their father's side. It all felt so hopeless. Even winning Lisa had not been enough compensation for what he had lost, and in any case he seemed to have messed that up too.

He went back to the lounge sofa, though he paid no attention at all to what was on television. Nothing could break into his gloomy thoughts.

Eleven

After the solemn three-hour vigil of Good Friday, Rosalind walked back across the churchyard with Keith Grey. Around them, the grass looked lushly green, patterned with daisies and speedwell, the ancient tombstones – burials here had ceased many years ago – softened with lichen and moss. 'This is going to need cutting soon,' she said. 'What usually happens about that?'

'Wilf Howard's looked after it for years,' the church-warden told her. 'Unfortunately he's laid low just now, with a bad back. But he'd be very unhappy if anyone else took over. I think we have to wait a bit and see how he does.'

'Does he get paid for it?'

'Why yes, though not a great deal. Pocket money. Though as he's only his pension to live on otherwise, that's not to be sniffed at.'

That seemed fair enough; but Rosalind suddenly thought of someone they could perhaps turn to if Wilf did not recover before the fastest growing period was on them – someone who would only want to take the work on temporarily, but for whom it might be a lifeline. She said nothing for the moment, but filed the thought away in her mind.

There were more than the usual number of people in the flower-scented, candle-shining church on Easter morning. Unlike her caller on Monday, most people seemed eager to hear the Easter message of hope, to cling to something positive in the surrounding grimness. For that hour or so, the joyful hymns seemed to drown out the chorus of misery, to shout out that there was always light in the dark.

On Easter Monday, Alastair announced that he was taking

Rosalind to the seaside. 'No foot-and-mouth there. We can walk on the beach.' So they did, taking Josh with them. They had fish and chips for lunch, and for those few hours left all their troubles behind.

Somehow it was harder to come back to the smoke that hung over the landscape, and the smell. 'Looks as though they've got that pyre started up at Black Fell,' Alastair observed as the car came within sight of the hill-top town.

'I'm going to a meeting about it tomorrow night,' Josh said suddenly from behind them.

Rosalind exchanged an astonished glance with Alastair. When had their son developed a social conscience? Or had it been there all the time and he had simply never let them know? Rosalind, who had been a fighter for causes all her life, had always been a little disappointed that neither of her children seemed to care much about the injustices of the world around them. On the other hand, she did not want either of them becoming entangled in the wilder fringes of the various protest movements, which as a girl she would probably have joined herself.

'What brought that on?' Rosalind asked, when her astonishment had subsided enough for speech.

'Oh, you know, someone spoke to me about it in a pub. They give off dioxins, you know, those pyres. Anyway, I said I'd go along.' There was a slight pause, then he asked casually, 'Will you be needing your car tomorrow night, Mum?'

This sudden turn of events would be something to share with Sophie tonight, thought Rosalind. The daily calls continued to leave her feeling utterly helpless in the face of Sophie's misery, but it was all she could do – to keep in touch and hope that by doing so she brought a small measure of comfort to the isolated young vet.

At Rose Cottage, Lisa too had felt the need to escape from the dale. 'Let's just go out somewhere, away from here – anywhere that isn't countryside,' she suggested to Scott as they sat at breakfast. But Scott did not even look up from his plate.

'I'm not in the mood,' he said. 'Besides, can't afford the petrol.'

'Your bike hardly uses any!'

He shrugged. 'Don't want to waste it.'

'Oh well, if you think giving me a ride out is wasting it, then that says it all!' Lisa stood up, making her chair scrape noisily over the tiles. 'Or are you saving it to give me a ride up to Black Fell tomorrow night?' She had spoken sarcastically, supposing she already knew the answer, but she could see, when at last he did look up, that he had no idea what she was talking about. 'For the protest meeting, about the disposal site.'

'Oh that! I told you what I thought about it. I've had enough of foot-and-mouth.'

'But not so much that you can't take one day to get right away from it!' She did not wait to hear his reply – if any – but simply marched out of the room. Scott continued to munch gloomily on his toast. He felt that Lisa simply did not understand, did not even begin to try to understand how wounded he felt, torn up from his roots and cast aside, as if he were worthless, as if his life had no meaning. She no longer seemed to want to try and give it meaning, for she had stopped coming to his bed at night. 'What's the point?' she'd asked when, nervously, obliquely, he'd challenged her. 'I have to do all the work. I don't believe I mean anything to you.'

It wasn't true, of course; she did mean something to him, a great deal – everything, or so he told himself. Yet he knew too that he could not feel fully happy and at ease, even with Lisa, without the acceptance of his family, without a future in the family farm which he had come to see was in his bloodstream, a part of him. Frozen out by them, he felt paralysed, as if some vital source of nourishment had been cut off, depriving him of energy and of any motivation for action. This was the first year, in all his life, when he had not been with them at Easter time. Worse, he had not heard anything from them; his mother, usually so careful to keep in touch, had not even rung his mobile to wish him happy Easter. On Sunday afternoon he had screwed up his courage to phone the farm, but no one had answered. True, she had treated him to lunch in the village cafe one day last week and for a moment that had soothed him; but she could do no more to heal the wound than anyone else. The hurt remained.

Black Fell village hall was already half full when Josh and Lisa reached it on Tuesday evening, even though they had arrived half an hour before the meeting was due to begin. Fate had indeed smiled on Josh; though his mother needed her car for a diocesan meeting, his father had allowed him to borrow the Focus, once he had extracted various promises about the way he drove, where he went and when he was likely to be home again.

So he had been able, in good time, to park triumphantly in front of Rose Cottage and usher Lisa into the car, holding the passenger door for her with a mature and worldly graciousness. It was unfortunate that the car stalled the moment he was ready to drive off, which caused an undignified scrabbling about with gears, clutch, brakes and ignition and had taken what seemed an embarrassingly long time to rectify, prompting Lisa to say, 'I was going to ask if this was your car, but I can see it's not.'

'Dad's,' growled Josh. Then he got everything properly coordinated and the car moved smoothly away. He drove rather more carefully than he might have done after that, for fear of further embarrassment.

At the hall, a tall young woman in a purple sweater came to greet them. 'Jackie, this is Josh,' Lisa introduced him. She had already told Josh about the young mother who was leading the protests against the disposal site. The two women then engaged themselves in a lengthy discussion about tactics and agendas, and Josh put on an appearance of interest, while shooting furtive glances at the other occupants of the hall. It was clear that this was a subject that roused strong emotions in the neighbourhood,

118

for there were representatives of every age group and every background here – students like himself and Lisa; young parents like Jackie, some with children in tow; people his parents' age; pensioners, some of whom hobbled only with difficulty into the room, even a middle-aged woman in a wheelchair.

About five minutes before the meeting was due to begin there was a commotion near the door and a man whom Josh recognized as their MP came into the room; he was already being harangued by an irate old man leaning on a stick. He was, Josh supposed, the nearest the protesters were likely to get to the authorities that had set up the site, and as such could expect a stormy reception. Since, as a loyal member of New Labour, he presumably had the ear of the government, he was also one of the few people who might be able to get some changes made to the plans, if not their scrapping altogether.

Lisa went to meet the man and led him to the table at the head of the room, where Jackie hammered on the noisy surface, waiting until the room fell into something approaching silence. 'Right, let's begin shall we? For those of you who don't know him, I'd like to introduce Ted Desmond, our member of parliament, who we hope is going to answer our questions and then take our concerns back to government. Have we got a first question then?'

The MP held up his hand. 'Just a moment! Can I begin by saying a few words?' There was a rumble of anger at that, and the man gave a conciliatory smile. 'I'd just like to fill in the background, so that you understand what we're doing and why the site was set up here in the first place. That is not to say that I will not take your concerns very seriously indeed, but I do feel you need to know precisely what lies behind the decision.'

He talked for far too long, Josh felt, having very quickly explained what was obvious – that there were far too many animal carcasses to be disposed of in too short a time, the rendering plants could not cope and disposal on individual farms was not an option when the numbers were so great and

119

the personnel to carry out the work so insufficient. He droned on for twenty minutes about 'regrettable necessity' and 'every precaution' and public health being the government's first concern. Many of his remarks drew further rumbles of anger from the audience, some only silenced with difficulty by Jackie who, Josh thought, was increasingly inclined to butt in and silence Ted Desmond instead.

At last he came to an end and a barrage of questions and objections burst out from the floor, so many all at once that Jackie had to bang on the table again. The MP adroitly took control at that point, giving every appearance that each question merited his careful consideration and would be dealt with accordingly. His responses were always too long, and mostly consisted of a tactful rejection of the arguments put to him; but when he finally left and the meeting began to break up into groups, still talking and arguing, Josh murmured to Lisa, 'Did I imagine it, or was he saying he agreed there shouldn't be any more burning at the site?'

'No, that's what I thought too. At least, I *think* that's what he was saying.'

'We've won then, haven't we?'

'No, we haven't. We don't want a site there at all. Weren't you listening? Burning's the most urgent problem, but it's certainly not the only one. But it's a start, I suppose.'

Josh glanced at his watch. It was nearly ten o'clock, and his father wanted the car back by half past at the latest. 'I'll run you home now, then we can go for a drink at the Drovers, if you like.'

'Oh, everyone's going to the Three Tuns over the road. Won't you come along?'

That would mean taking the car back very late, and being unable to drink as well, since he would still have to drive home. Could he deliver an ultimatum to Lisa, to come with him now or be without her lift?

'Jackie'll run me back afterwards, if you've got to go.'

That decided him; he was staying. He would face his father later and risk his anger. He left the car where he

120

had parked it, at the edge of the hall car park close to a street lamp, and followed the others across the road.

It was not an entirely satisfactory evening. He had to watch his companions becoming increasingly convivial while he sipped an orange juice; and they talked so much and with such passion that he found it difficult to join in. He felt excluded by a combination of shyness, sobriety and the fact that these people had all known one another for some time, where he had only just met most of them.

But at last closing time arrived, and he and Lisa said goodnight and walked back together to the car park. He went to unlock the passenger door, and came to a shocked halt. 'Oh, shit!'

'What's the matter?'

He showed her. Along the side of the car was a long dent, marked with scratches. 'Someone's kicked it in. Oh God, what am I going to do? Dad'll kill me!' If only he'd gone straight home, he thought. He felt angry with himself for his weakness, angrier still with Lisa for delaying him.

She slid her arm into his. 'I'll come with you and explain,' she offered.

The feel of her so near to him, the scent of her perfume, her warmth, calmed him down – or rather, replaced anger with some rather sweeter commotion. They got in the car and he drove back to Meadhope, where she did indeed insist on coming into the house with him. They went straight to the lounge, where his father was dozing over the *Guardian*, and Josh confessed at once. Lisa said, 'It's all my fault, Mr Maclaren. I insisted on staying for a drink with the others. Josh wanted to come straight home, and of course he didn't drink anything, but he knew I couldn't get home without him.' That bit wasn't true, of course, but Josh was grateful for it.

'I'd better come and look,' said Alastair. All three went out to the drive, at the very moment Rosalind's car turned into it. Just what I need, Josh thought gloomily – a family meeting. He knew his parents were displeased, but they were fair-minded enough to know it wasn't really his fault, and at last let him go to walk Lisa home.

'What happens now?' Josh asked. 'About the disposal site, I mean?'

'We give it a day or two to see if they're going to take any notice of what we've said.'

'Did I hear Jackie say she'd been picketing the site?'

'Yes, a few of them have. I might join them if they don't scale it all down. Certainly if they go on burning up there. Would you join us if that happens?'

'I'm back at uni next week,' he told her with real regret. 'But any weekend I'm back, of course I'll join you. But maybe it'll all be over soon.'

'I hope so,' said Lisa. 'But I doubt it.'

Outside the guest house Lisa gave an exclamation under her breath and stopped. She had seen, coming towards them, a slim dark figure whom she clearly recognized. Josh saw it was the boy he had taken to be her brother. Now he wondered, the more so when he saw the expression on the lad's face as he came nearer. 'Who's that?' Josh asked in an undertone.

Lisa shrugged, then muttered a hasty goodnight and hurried towards the door. Josh was about to call after her, but the door had slammed shut behind her. Turning, he saw that the boy had almost reached him. He decided it might be better not to wait and see what was going to happen next and with a brief wave – why did I do that? he wondered – slipped into the lane and scuttled home. He would have to phone Lisa to see if she wanted to meet him one night for a drink; or should he simply hope he might bump into her again?

Lisa had only got halfway up the stairs when Scott came in. He called after her. 'Who was that?'

Lisa turned. 'Who was who?'

'You know quite well. The guy I saw you with just now, outside.'

'I don't see what business it is of yours. But if you must

122

know, that's Josh Maclaren, the vicar's son. He gave me a lift tonight. He's helping with the protests.' She wondered what Scott had been doing – he hardly ever went out – but didn't ask. That would be to imply she had a right to know, something she didn't want him to feel about her. 'It was a good meeting,' she added. 'I think we might be getting somewhere.'

'Oh, hooray for you! I bet that makes you feel good.'

She swung swiftly away from his sarcasm, running up to her room without even a goodnight. Scott stomped up the stairs after her, with the weight of the world on his shoulders.

After Lisa had gone out this evening he had decided he needed some fresh air and gone out for a walk, half hoping he would bump into a friend who would perhaps offer to buy him a drink. Closed in gloomy thoughts, he was startled to hear a voice call, 'All right, Scott?' It was a friend of his father's, returning home from the pub with a slight roll in his step. 'You not gone with them then?' Scott had stared at him blankly. 'Spain. That's where they've gone, isn't it? I thought that's what Dave said. First holiday in years. Do them good. But you'll have better things to do than go away with your parents,' he added, with what was clearly meant to be understanding. Then he went on his way, apparently not aware of any reason other than preference why Scott should not have gone on holiday with his family, nor suspecting either that Scott had known nothing about it.

It was like a blow to his stomach. A holiday, in the middle of foot-and-mouth, after all that had happened! They never went on holiday. And now, to go away without him, without even telling him . . . He had not thought he could hurt any more, but he did now, with a sharp agony. His mother – the one person he had thought had steadfastly, faithfully, continued to love him through all this – hers was the worst betrayal, for she must have known last week that they were going away, but she had said nothing, nothing at all.

Feeling as if the skin had been flayed from his body, exposing every nerve end to the air, he had gone on his way. Now he was glad to see no one he knew, though he would dearly have loved to be able to get thoroughly drunk, all by himself. Instead he had returned to the guest house just in time to see Lisa, the one glimmer of light in the darkness of his life, making her way home in the company of some trendy student type he had never seen before – and clearly enjoying it. She had at least not snogged him before they parted, but Scott had no way of knowing if she had done so earlier. He only had her word for it that this guy had simply been her means of getting to and from the meeting – and how was it possible to trust anyone any longer? If she wanted to punish him for not coming with her, then she had succeeded. Now, when he most needed comfort, she had deliberately shut him out.

Twelve

Josh returned to university having made no further progress with Lisa at all, though he had been welcomed to join her with a group of others in the Drovers one evening. She did at least promise to email him about what was happening at the disposal site. They were talking now of setting up a full-scale picket, whether the burning continued or not. 'I'll see if I can get back odd weekends,' Josh promised. After all, during the week, Lisa would be too busy with her studies to take things too far with anyone else; or so he hoped. He had tried asking her about the youth staying at Rose Cottage, but it had not been easy when all her friends were there and she had either not heard him or pretended not to hear.

As for Scott, he withdrew more and more into himself. He hardly spoke to Lisa at all, which just made her give up on him altogether. On the Monday Lisa went back to college, he had a call on his mobile from his mother. He was tempted simply to switch it off, but he finally answered. 'Can we meet for a coffee in my break, Scott love?' she had asked. He was tempted to say no, and then to tell her why not, but he found himself mumbling a grudging compliance, and at ten thirty he found himself seated opposite her in the otherwise empty cafe. He watched her as she gave the order, wondering how long it would be before she broke the news to him about the holiday, and how she would do it.

She said nothing, simply began to ask after him, what he had been doing over Easter, how things were with Lisa, sympathizing when he indicated, obliquely, that they were not going well. If he had not known what she was keeping back, he would have suspected nothing, though he might have wondered where she had got that rejuvenating tan. As it was, he noted the little signs of nervousness – a slight tremor of the hands, so that she fumbled with her coffee cup; a failure, for more than a passing moment, to meet his gaze.

Before long their conversation – if such a one-sided affair could be called a conversation – dwindled into silence. Aware of something odd about her son's mood, Linda did look at him then, with a puzzled, questioning look. Scott said baldly, 'I know. I know you all went off on holiday, to Spain. I saw Bradley Peart.'

If Linda had been in any doubt about her son's deep hurt, she had only to look at his face, hear the raw pain in his voice as he spoke those unequivocally accusing words. She blushed, like a girl caught out in some misdeed, while Scott watched her squirm without pity. First she merely said, 'Oh!' Then she said in a rush, 'I didn't want you to be hurt. I thought if you didn't know—'

'How could I not know something was up? You didn't even phone me at Easter! A whole week, and not a word. And then to find out from someone else like that!'

Linda reached across the table to caress his hand, but he snatched it back. 'I'm sorry, Scott. I'm really sorry. I've cocked up big time, haven't I? But I really did mean it for the best, truly I did.'

'I wouldn't mind, only you never go on holiday, never!'

'The compensation money came through, so we thought, with no animals left . . .'

'But . . . the money . . . that's so we – you – can restock.'

'It was a cheap holiday. But in any case,' she added more slowly, 'your dad's still talking of selling up, when all this is over.'

All thought of her duplicity, of secret holidays, was swept from his mind. 'Selling up? Selling Middle Byers? But what will you do? Where would you go?'

'I don't know, Scott. I really don't know. This is all

such a mess.' She was staring down at her hands, which lay clenched together on the table.

He felt a sudden pity for her, caught in the middle, trying to be the peacemaker, the conciliator for them all. Perhaps she had deserved a holiday, if no one else had. 'Did you have a good time in Spain?'

'Yes, yes, it was nice to get right away.' She hesitated, and then said slowly, as if fearing she was breaking a confidence, 'I did sort of hope your dad might come back differently – you know, ready to make up. Thinking more positively about the farm – and you.'

'But he hasn't?'

She shook her head sadly. 'It doesn't look like it, so far.' She took another sip of her coffee. 'Sheila said she thought the number of cases was dropping a bit.'

Scott had no need to ask what she was talking about; and though on the whole he tried to avoid watching the news or looking at papers, he somehow still knew the answer. 'Maybe. But then there can't be that many farms haven't already been hit, one way or another. Not round here anyway. It seems it's still getting worse in Cumbria, and down in the West Country. Still, at least it hasn't got any further up the dale. Yet.'

'If the wind carries it, then it's mostly the other way.'

'And if people carry it, then no one much is moving up the dale. Still, no one seems to know.'

'Maybe we never will.'

'If they don't find out, they can't stop it happening again.'

'I think that's why your dad's talking of selling up. He couldn't face ever having to go through all this again.' And that included his break with Scott – without that, everything would have been very much easier to bear, for Scott would have been there among them, one of a loving family giving each other support and comfort.

When she arrived home that afternoon, slightly earlier than usual, Linda realized as she stepped into the kitchen that Dave was on the phone. Some instinct made her walk very quietly across the room to the just-open door that led into the hall. She put up her hand to push it further open, and then stopped, listening. 'But how soon can you restock, that's what I want to know?'

A long silence followed, broken by an occasional murmur, and then Dave said, 'Right! I understand! Thanks,' and Linda heard the click as the call ended. She stepped into the hall. Dave appeared to be pushing a few papers together on the table on which the phone stood – notes? He looked round. 'Hello there. Good day?'

Though she met Scott quite often, she had only mentioned that fact to his father once before, some time ago, in the hope that Dave might show signs of relenting towards his son. Now, she thought, might be the moment to try again. If that call had indeed meant that Dave was, at least speculatively, considering restocking the farm when regulations allowed, then this might indicate that he was mellowing, that the holiday had after all led him to look at the past months in a different way. 'I met Scott for a coffee,' she said.

'They must have been glad to have you back,' Dave said, as if she had not spoken. So, she thought, nothing's changed there at least.

At the rectory, term-time calm was restored, though only on the surface. Both Rosalind and Alastair were deeply concerned about Sophie, plunged right into the heart of the crisis in Cumbria, for whom their daily phone calls were some sort of lifeline. Then, a week after Easter, Sophie suddenly became unavailable. She not only ceased to phone them herself, but did not answer her mobile either, though they left persistent messages. After a week of this, Rosalind became distraught. 'What if she's ill, all alone with no one to care for her? Or if it's all got too much for her . . . ?'

Alastair hugged her. She knew he understood precisely what she was saying, knew what she feared. 'She's tough as old boots, our Sophie. She'll be OK. Perhaps she's back at university now.'

'Then why hasn't she phoned? Or answered our calls?'

'Too busy working for exams, perhaps.' He paused, and she knew then that he shared her fears. 'When you phone tonight, forget the neutral messages. Tell her we're desperate for news, ask if she's sick or suicidal. Maybe that'll prod her into ringing back.'

So Rosalind did just that. 'Sophie? We're worried sick. Are you still alive? Are you well? Please phone us!' It was the sort of desperate, hysterical message she would not normally have dreamed of leaving; but it worked. Within half an hour the phone rang and Sophie's voice came on the line, though she sounded so different from the anguished girl of the past weeks that Rosalind almost failed to recognize her. She was laughing, breaking off what sounded like a teasing remark thrown at someone else. Wherever she was now, she was quite clearly no longer alone.

'We were getting a bit anxious about you, not having heard for a while,' said Rosalind, trying not to sound reproachful. 'But you sound pretty happy.'

'Sorry not to phone, Mum. I've been a bit busy. Well, you know how it is.'

That, Rosalind thought, was precisely what she did not know, since it was clear that something in her daughter's life had changed. 'Are you back at university?'

'Oh no, not yet. I'm still in Cumbria, in the same place.' There was a sudden noisy burst of talk behind her.

'Have they found you a fellow lodger then?'

'Yes. Two in fact. It's so much better, Mum. We can all get drunk together at the end of the day.'

That explained the hilarity, Rosalind supposed. They talked a little longer, but Sophie was clearly anxious to get back to whatever she had been doing – Rosalind suspected that getting drunk was only incidental to it, and by no means the whole story. In fact, by the time Sophie rang off, she had a distinct sense that more had been left unsaid than said. Still, she could bear to have her curiosity unsatisfied if it meant her daughter was happier, or so she told herself. In reality she was eaten up with curiosity.

*   *   *

129

April turned to May. The election, rescheduled for early June, drew nearer. There were meetings – marred by rancour and ill-temper – in selected urban areas, though none in the blighted dale. Spring came into full bloom, but the dale and its people seemed frozen, waiting for hope to return to the empty fields. Flowers proliferated in neglected meadows and pastures, the bright young green of the trees turned darker, stronger; the grass in the churchyard grew taller and more lush. Wilf Howard was still laid up, and even he agreed that someone would need to be brought in temporarily, to maintain the churchyard as it should be. With the approval of the PCC standing committee, Rosalind made her way to Rose Cottage one Tuesday morning. Scott, with nothing to get up for, was still in bed. 'More than time the lazy sod was up,' Elaine Robson said, admitting Rosalind. 'I'll go and fetch him.' Rosalind suspected she would enjoy doing it.

Scott, dragged from the heavy, unrestful slumber into which he'd fallen after waking too early, grunted at Elaine's sharp command and slid from the bed. What on earth could the rector want with him? He pulled on his clothes, which he'd left in a scrumpled heap on the floor, and then made his way, unwashed and unshaven, down the stairs to the residents' lounge, where he found Rosalind idly turning the pages of a magazine.

She put it down and gestured towards a nearby armchair. 'I'm hoping you can get us out of a tight spot. But it may be you've got other commitments by now, in which case I'm too late.'

He said nothing, simply wondered what she was talking about. Was this a roundabout way of luring him to church?

'I don't know if you know Wilf Howard? Used to look after the churchyard for us. Well, he's laid up just now. So you see, we need someone to step into the breach, just for this season. I did think you might be the person. The only trouble is, we can't pay much. Five pounds an hour, but it's only five hours a week.'

From his present, utterly penniless, viewpoint that seemed

almost like riches. But he was wary of appearing too enthusiastic. 'I had thought I'd go back to Darlington to look for work. Or somewhere.'

'And that would be much better paid, I know. I do understand. On the other hand, something like this would fill a gap, if that's what you wanted, until you know what you want to do.' Implied, he knew, was, 'Until your father comes round'. But he was still not going to rush into it.

She stood up. 'Think about it. You'd be doing us a tremendous favour if you would say yes. But it has to be right for you too.' She began to move towards the door.

'Mrs Maclaren!' Was that how you addressed a lady vicar?

She turned back. 'Rosalind, please!'

'Rosalind. OK then. Yes, I'll do it for you.'

'You don't know how grateful I am!' she said, smiling broadly. 'You can almost see that grass growing. When would you like to come and have a look at the set-up? There's a fair bit of equipment.'

'Now?' he suggested. 'I'm not doing anything.'

On the way to the churchyard, Rosalind said, 'It would probably be a good idea to go and have a word with Wilf. Apart from anything else, that would make him feel he's not being sidelined.'

'I'll go round there this afternoon,' Scott promised. Suddenly there were things to be done, responsibilities for him to take up; already he felt more alert, more vigorous.

By the time Rosalind made her way home, just an hour later, Scott had already begun work, the subdued roar of the large mower filling the air as he steered it around the tombstones. He did not look exactly happy, but he certainly had the purposeful air of someone with a useful role to fulfil. By the end of the day, there was enough of a change for Alastair to comment on it when he came home. 'So he agreed, the Emerson lad?'

'On present showing, he's a good worker too.'

'So all you need now is to get his father speaking to him?' he asked as he hung up his coat. 'Or does that have to wait till the autumn, for the sake of the church-yard?'

'If I could think of a way to get those two speaking to each other again, I'd do it now. But Dave Emerson's a stubborn man. An unhappy one too, of course, which is the root of the trouble. It's so sad, just at the time when having your family round you really matters, to be faced with a horrible row like this. Especially when there's no need for it.'

'Maybe all he needs is time.'

'I hope so. The trouble is, the longer it's left, the more he'll feel he's losing face if he gives in, even if he isn't really angry any more.' She linked her arm through Alastair's. 'What about your day then?'

'Ah, now, that brings me to the bee in my bonnet: holidays.'

'Let's talk about it over supper. It's all ready.'

Later, at the kitchen table, Alastair returned to the subject. 'Everyone's putting in for their holidays, and I still don't know which dates we want. What about it? You need a break and so do I. It's your birthday at the end of August. If I can't drag you away sooner, we could go away then.'

'What about your mother? We were going to stay with her some time.'

'That's not a holiday, even for me. No, I can do that separately.'

'Well, we can hardly go to the cottage this year.' Some years before they had taken out a mortgage on a cottage in the heart of the Yorkshire dales, which they rented out as a holiday cottage and planned to use for their retirement one day – either as somewhere to live, or to sell and put the proceeds towards a retirement home elsewhere. It was their security, for when they would no longer be living in the accommodation that went with Rosalind's job. But at the moment it was simply a drain on their resources, unlettable with foot-and-mouth all around it and not even suitable for their own use while there was such a risk to the countryside. 'Pity we didn't opt for the seaside bungalow.'

'Yes, Bide-a-Wee would have been just the place.' It was an old joke – they had walked past a poky bungalow with just that name on the outskirts of Southport many years ago. 'There, my dream home!' Alastair had exclaimed.

Now, Rosalind giggled. Their eyes met across the table, an intimate glance which had in it all the many things they had shared, the thoughts they each knew the other was thinking, the memories, the tenderness. That was, Rosalind thought, one thing about a long marriage – there were many times when words were not only unnecessary but impossible, because they could never express the complicated intricacies of shared emotion and memory. At such times it was only in silence that they could fully communicate with one another. An outsider, looking on, would think atrophy had long ago set in, that they were bored, that they no longer had anything to say to one another. But it was not like that at all. Some things were simply beyond words.

They resumed eating. After a moment Rosalind said, 'Well then, are you going to give me a surprise holiday for my birthday?' She would be forty-nine in August.

'I just might. A city break somewhere perhaps. Wait and see!'

'You'll—'

'I know, I'll have to give you enough warning to arrange cover. I know the score.' He took another mouthful, then said, 'Your father would cover for you, if you wanted, wouldn't he? I know you didn't like to ask him when we were at Coldwell – it wouldn't have been much of a holiday for him there, or for your mother either. But Meadhope's different.'

'Not in the middle of foot-and-mouth, it isn't,' Rosalind pointed out.

'Maybe the footpaths will be open again by then. In any case, your father doesn't walk so much these days, does he? We could leave them a car. They'd be happy enough pottering around in that, if one of your brothers did the long haul up here.'

'Maybe. I'll think about it.' Alastair was right, she thought; her father would love to feel he could still be useful.

Thirteen

Lisa was contemptuous about Scott's new occupation. 'Call that a job! It's pocket money, that's all.'

'Better than nothing,' he said, clearly wounded by her attitude.

But she had to admit that it brought about a change in him. He suddenly looked brighter, happier, more like the Scott she remembered from last year. He clearly enjoyed the work, even took a real pride in it. Within a week of starting work, the churchyard was looking immaculate. If, as sometimes happened, the machines he used broke down, he – unlike Wilf – had enough skill to repair them. Coming to the work with fresh eyes, he found more effective ways to tackle some of the tasks, though, mindful of Rosalind's words, he continued to visit the old man and even made a pretence of taking advice from him, though he rather doubted that Wilf would ever be fit enough to come back to work. Though he earned very little, he made sure that most of his earnings went to Lisa's mother. Unfortunately, Elaine was less than impressed. 'That won't go far towards your keep,' she said.

'I know.' He coloured uncomfortably, in the way she often made him do; he could never feel quite at ease in her presence.

'Still, better than nothing. Thanks.' It was not exactly approval, but it was as near as he was likely to come to it for the time being. That was the drawback with this little job – it simply didn't pay enough. He would have to think of something else, unless his father came round quickly.

The next day, while he was working in the churchyard,

135

something happened that suggested a way of making more money. For a moment or two he wrestled with his conscience; then he went to the rectory to see Rosalind.

'I've had an idea,' he said as she admitted him to the study. 'It's like this: yesterday when I was cutting the grass, some woman came up and asked would I like to earn a bit cutting her grass too.'

'That's good! I'm sure you could do with a bit more.'

'No, hang on a minute! She wanted me to use the big mower. She lives in that house just next to the church. She's got a lot of grass and usually gets someone in, but she didn't want to bring outsiders into the dale, the way things are. I know it wouldn't be right to use the church mower on the side. But if the money went to the church . . .'

Rosalind was impressed by the lad's integrity. She knew that many people in his position would simply have taken the mower, quietly, through to the adjacent garden and then pocketed the proceeds. 'That's a good idea. Except that you ought to have something yourself for your work. You should take half anyway. As for the rest – yes, well, the church could always do with funds. Or maybe for the time being it should go to the farmers' fund.' She knew that pleased him. As he left, she added, 'Feel free to take on other work too, just so long as the churchyard has priority and you take care of the equipment. Same terms, of course.'

By the end of the week, he had enough work to keep him busy full-time, even allowing him to earn sufficient to put a smile on Elaine's face. 'You've got more to you than I thought,' Elaine conceded when he looked in at Friday lunch time to make an extra payment towards his lodging. 'An enterprising lad. I suppose that's what they call diversification.'

Something chimed in Scott's head. Diversification: machinery, his own mechanical skills; a vision of his father approving, welcoming him home; the two of them working together for the good of the farm and the family . . . He was seized by a sense of excitement, hope, anticipation. Steady on! he told himself. Think it over first. Don't rush

136

in too soon and spoil everything. He grinned at Elaine. 'Big tycoon, that's me,' he said.

On his way back to the churchyard for his afternoon's work, he met Lisa in the lane. 'Fancy going out for a drink tonight?' he asked. It felt very good to be able to invite her to do something so normal, so ordinary as to go out for a Friday-night drink; to have it in his power to restore their relationship to what it once had been.

She shook her head. 'I'm going on the picket line, up at the site. You should come too.'

The light faded from his face. He grimaced. 'Not me. I've told you what I think about that.'

'Scott, you ought to care about it! Just think of all those rotting carcasses they're bringing in. Think of the risk of infection. All right, I know it's too late for your farm, but there are others that haven't been affected yet—'

'Do you think I don't know that? If anyone should know about the risk of infection, it's me. And I'm keeping right away from any diseased carcasses. I don't want anyone accusing me ever again of spreading disease around. Those people on the picket line up there, they're asking for trouble.'

'Not if they clean up afterwards,' said Lisa quickly, though it was an aspect of the protests that had not occurred to her.

'Oh yes, and how many do? Have you got disinfectant up there?'

'There's a strip across the road, with straw and stuff,' she said, but he could see that she was faltering.

'For vehicles, yes, but that'll be it. How many of that lot up there wash their shoes before they leave, or change their clothes? None, I'll bet.' Suddenly anger flared in him. 'You lot think you're so high-minded, with all your protests, but you don't begin to understand what it's like, what it's really like! You haven't a clue what farmers are up against.' He felt a tremor of astonishment that he should dare to criticize Lisa, for whom until now he would have lain down so she could walk all over him. Suddenly what he thought mattered, as it had not done before; his opinions had a new validity – above all, he *had* opinions, thought out by himself, without prompting from anyone else.

Rosalind, on her way home from a prolonged and depressing visit to a new resident at the old people's home, came round the corner at that moment to find her way blocked by the furiously arguing young couple. Scott had his mouth open, on the brink of hurling some further retort at his companion, but he closed it again, swung round and strode rapidly away, soon disappearing round the next corner. Lisa stood watching him, with a mixture of dismay and misery on her small face. Then she glanced at Rosalind. 'Men!'

'I'm sorry – bad timing,' said Rosalind.

The girl shrugged. 'It wouldn't have made any difference. Nothing's right for him at the moment.'

It was clear that she had no wish to discuss the matter further, so Rosalind went on her way, making a detour to Meadhope's small supermarket to stock up on food, since Josh had suddenly turned up this morning at a time that must have meant a very early start for a student. 'Just fancied a weekend at home,' he had said airily when, abruptly summoned, she had gone to meet him from the station. She wondered now what his real motive was, and if he might tell her over lunch.

Passing the churchyard on her way home, she saw Scott trudging behind the mower as it roared its way among the gravestones. He stopped to refuel it when it fell silent. On impulse she went over to him, concerned about how he might be feeling after the quarrel she had overheard. 'Lovely afternoon, for a change. How are things?'

He straightened. 'OK, thanks.' He did not look particularly troubled – on the contrary, there was a new brightness in his eyes. He paused, in the manner of someone wondering whether or not to say more. Then he went on, 'You know this mower? The people you got it from – do they make other stuff? Other bigger stuff, I mean?'

'I really don't know. It was here when I arrived, so I had nothing to do with buying it. I suppose one of the churchwardens would know. Are you in search of something bigger and better then?'

'Well, sort of.' He told her what was on his mind and she listened intently.

'You might find the information you're looking for on the Internet. Have you got access to a computer?' There was certainly a computer at Rose Cottage, but perhaps having fallen out with Lisa he would not find it easy to ask for use of it. 'I tell you what – come round to the rectory some time and have a look on my computer. You could also check out what grants might be available – I've already got some information on that. Give me a ring – or no, I'll ring you when I've checked what's in the diary. I've got your number.'

She reached the rectory to find Josh on the extension phone in the hall. He put down the receiver as she came in, but his expression was ecstatic. 'Good news?' she asked.

'Oh, I'm needed on the picket line up at the burial site,' he told her. 'I'm going up there this afternoon.' He did not say that it was Lisa who'd asked him to come, that she had at last contacted him instead of the other way round, and that for the first time she had willingly involved him.

'Am I about to get a request to borrow the car? Because the answer's no. I've a round of hospital visits to make this afternoon.'

He was disappointed. He had made no promises to Lisa – they had even agreed to meet at the bus stop, for one of the four buses a day that ran from Meadhope to Black Fell – but he had hoped he would be in a position to offer her a lift home at the end of the day, when the buses ceased to run.

'In any case,' his mother was saying now, 'I don't think I'd be happy at the thought of the car being parked up there all afternoon, even if I didn't need it. Too much potential for damage. But what I will do is drop you off on my way to Durham, if you can wait until after lunch.'

'Thanks, Mum,' he said. Then added casually, 'Could you give Lisa a lift too?'

So that was it! Rosalind studied her son's face and

wondered if he was in any way implicated in the quarrel she had witnessed this morning. She rather hoped not, since Scott Emerson had troubles enough of his own without having to cope with a rival for his girlfriend's attentions – and Rosalind certainly didn't want her own son to be that rival. It was, of course, much more likely that Josh simply had hopes which had not yet even begun to be realized. After all, he had not been at home very much recently, and not having a job he had little spending money for going out in the evening. On the other hand, a gentle warning might be in order. 'I think there's someone else in the picture as far as Lisa's concerned,' she said. 'Just in case you have any hopes in that direction.'

She saw Josh blush fiercely. 'We're just friends,' he said. 'Anyway, it's up to Lisa.' But for a moment he felt downcast. Could his mother be right? There was that guy at Rose Cottage. But Josh had never seen them together, nor had Lisa ever mentioned a boyfriend. Besides, if they were an item, he would surely have been with her at the meeting and on the picket line. Hope restored, Josh phoned Lisa to tell her the plan and then ran upstairs to consider what to wear – something casual, of course, something that wouldn't spoil if he got muddy, but something whose colour flattered him, and the shape too.

An hour later, too excited to eat more than a sandwich for lunch, he was ready before his mother even had the car out of the garage. When they picked up Lisa, she got into the back. Josh longed to move from the front seat to join her, but was too afraid of rejection to do it in front of his mother, just in case Lisa said something hurtful, however subtly. Rosalind dropped them at the end of the road that led to the burial site and they walked together towards the entrance, where two police vans were parked. Just at that moment a convoy of trucks arrived, stinking from their decaying cargo. Josh retched at the stench. This was not after all going to be an unrelieved pleasure. But he would stick it out, for the possibilities the situation offered.

*   *   *

Rosalind returned from her hospital visits to find a phone message from one of the helpline volunteers. He couldn't manage his full evening session, so would she please find someone else to fill in? She felt irritated, both at the short notice and the fact that it was passed on to her. She knew from past experience that this would most likely mean she would be the one to fill the gap, since no one else would be available. Unfortunately the early enthusiasm of the volunteers was wearing off, at the same time as the number of calls dwindled. She herself found her sessions very boring, but was aware that there were still people for whom it was a first resort in a crisis.

She put the problem to Alastair when he came in. 'I've phoned round everyone I could think of,' she said, 'but no one's available. To be honest, a good many of them are losing enthusiasm for doing it. We've lost three volunteers this past week.'

'I suppose it's inevitable there'd be some cooling off. Do you still need the helpline?'

'I think so, yes. The calls are different now, and there aren't so many. A lot of them are about practical things, on the surface at least. Farmers tearing their hair out because they've had yet another sheaf of instructions from DEFRA about disinfecting, or animal movements, or whatever, mostly contradicting everything they've been told before. Then they try the official helplines and no one can give them a straight answer. There's still an awful lot of anger. But it's actually rather harder than it was to know how to help.'

'Do you need some feedback as to what sort of help would be best, if there are any changes you need to make?'

'I was talking about it to Daphne Wynyard when I was at Ashburn last Sunday. She certainly felt we were still serving a purpose.'

'Maybe you should ask her to volunteer.'

'I thought of that. But would she be worried about moving about, carrying infection?'

'She's been going to her Countryside Alliance meetings, hasn't she? Didn't you say she'd been to see someone about organizing something big for next year? In person, not just via email?'

'Yes. Yes, you're right. And come to think of it, I don't think there are any farms with animals left in Ashburn.'

So before leaving to fill the gap on the helpline, Rosalind telephoned Daphne Wynyard to ask if she would be willing to add to the number of volunteers. She began by explaining how complicated many of the requests for help had become. 'It's getting hard for most of us to disentangle it all. Usually it means chasing up some official and then getting yet more conflicting advice.'

'Then I tell you what,' said Daphne, before she'd even reached the main point of her call. 'Put me on the line. God knows I've got time on my hands. I could spend the best part of a day on your helpline. I've got experience of DEFRA – all right, I know it *was* MAFF, but I can't tell one from t'other.' The old Ministry of Agriculture, Fisheries and Food had recently been restructured and renamed the Department for the Environment, Food and Rural Affairs. 'I'd say I'm just what you need. I could start tomorrow. Not all the time – I've still got horses to feed and exercise, even if I can't take them out. But what I could do is take over the organization if you like, run the thing. I'd keep them on their toes.'

Rosalind did not doubt it, but was not sure she wanted to go that far. But it was with a sense of relief that she set out for her unplanned evening session. Of one thing she was quite sure; if anyone could find a way through the jungle of conflicting paperwork that faced farmers in the aftermath of the crisis, then Daphne was the one.

Before leaving the house, she also phoned Scott on his mobile and arranged for him to come to the rectory on Monday evening. 'I'll be around if you need help,' she offered, sensing that he lacked computer skills.

Rosalind returned home that evening just as Josh, having gone on to the Three Tuns in Black Fell with Lisa, reached home. He was in a euphoric state; though Lisa had not exactly suggested that they might become an item, she had certainly been more attentive than ever before, more

142

inclined to single him out in conversation or sit close to him. She had even allowed him to touch her arm, lay a hand over hers. Tomorrow they would be picketing again. It was still not going to be a pleasant experience, but he had high hopes all the same. It was just a pity that he had to go back to uni on Sunday. He was counting the days to the summer vacation, just over a month away now.

On Wednesday the following week, Linda Emerson, just home from work, said to Dave, 'I saw Scott today. He's had an idea – he's thought it out very carefully. He asked me to put it to you. I think he's got something.'

'I wish you'd stop meeting him like that. You know what I think about it. You're deliberately going against my wishes.'

'Scott's my son as much as you're my husband. I'm not going to behave as if he'd died, even if you are.'

'If he'd died I could remember him kindly. This is worse.'

Linda's skin crawled with horror. 'Worse than him being dead? Oh, Dave, you don't mean that!'

'Don't I? How come you know what I think better than I do?'

'At least listen to what he told me! I'm sure you'll be impressed. It's an idea for when we restock the farm.'

'Who said anything about restocking? And even if I do, there'll be no place in it for him. You know that. Nor his ideas either. So don't waste your breath on it.'

'All I know is you're the most stupid, pig-headed man that ever was born. God knows why I married you!' She stamped out of the room, slamming the door behind her. It was only later, looking back, that she realized he'd said *even if I do*. So he was about to change his mind about restocking, she thought. If only there were such small but hopeful signs that he might change his mind about Scott!

Moor Farm was at last fully disinfected of the disease it had never had – the tests on their slaughtered animals had indeed proved negative, the final cruel blow for the Oldfields. 'But at least we're officially clear now,' Ben said during his daily call to Sally. 'Officially clear of something we've never had – Kafka had nothing on this for weirdness. When are you coming home?'

'Today?' she suggested.

It took her longer than she expected to pack, for she had somehow accumulated far more in her stay at Rose Cottage than she had realized. She paid Elaine all the money that was due, and thanked her with real warmth for her welcome. 'You've made me so comfortable. I could never have been happy away from Ben, but you've made it bearable and even pleasant.'

'And you've got my web site going, so I'm ready for off as soon as this horrible epidemic's over. I can't thank you enough. You've got a real flair for this sort of thing. I reckon you could have quite a little business if you wanted to. There are a lot of technophobes out there who need help.'

'You could have something there,' said Sally thoughtfully. Then Ben was at the door, and she was in his arms. Before long they were driving up the hill, familiar yet unfamiliar, turning between the Moor Farm gateposts, bumping along the track across the empty fields towards the empty farmyard.

Ben stopped the car and turned off the ignition. Then he turned to Sally and they kissed, long and lingeringly. 'Welcome home, darling,' he said.

Indoors, the house seemed cold, as if it had been empty for a long time. When Sally commented on this, Ben said, 'Without you, it *was* empty. Now it's a home again.'

He carried Sally's luggage upstairs and left her to unpack while he went to prepare their evening meal. She took her time, savouring this return to her home, her place. She was going to have to do some cleaning soon, she thought; Ben had done his best, but he didn't have her eye for dust.

Downstairs, she heard the phone ring. Some time later, when she went downstairs, Ben was still talking, though he soon rang off. 'What was all that about?' she asked.

144

'Young Vicky from across the road. She's trying to get the farm records on the Internet. She's a bright lass, but some of it's beyond her. I've been helping when I can.'

'Perhaps I can give her a hand too.' Then she added, 'You know, Ben, Dave Emerson won't be the only farmer who'd benefit from getting some IT skills. It's not just farmers either. I've been helping Elaine Robson, as you know. And the other day Rosalind Maclaren asked me to help improve the parish web site.'

'Did she now?' He fell silent as their eyes met. 'I think I know what you're thinking. It's quite a thought.' Now his eyes, like hers, were shining.

Fourteen

Josh came home once more before the end of term, though he saw little of his parents or the rectory as he spent most of the weekend on the picket line with Lisa. Progress was still painfully slow, but not slow enough for him to give up hope – now and then there was even a hug or a kiss to encourage him, though he feared they were simply expressions of high spirits or mild affection rather than anything warmer.

There was even less progress as far as the burial site was concerned. In spite of ceaseless, noisy and even occasionally violent picketing, trucks continued to bring in carcasses day and night for disposal. By now, they were mostly the result of contiguous culling in other parts of the country, for it was these animals that now formed the bulk of the slaughter.

The general election took place in the second week of June, with predictable results. Ted Desmond was returned to his ministerial seat and the vague promises he had made – on the question of the disposal site, about bringing broadband to the dale's computer users – melted away in the daily business of government.

Then examinations intervened, and Josh could not spare the time to come home any longer. His sister was also busy with exams, having returned to university some weeks before. These final exams were the more vital as, having found a place with a small Lake District mixed animal veterinary practice, she was eager to take it up as soon as possible. Rosalind wondered if there was some deeper significance in the location of this 'dream practice', as her daughter described it. Could it have anything to do with one of the laughing companions of her stay in Cumbria? Sophie still sounded astonishingly happy; for her, it was almost as if the traumatic events of the spring had never happened.

It was not so easy for Rosalind's parishioners to put the disease behind them, because they all knew it was not over. Though the number of new cases might be falling, there were still outbreaks every few days in other parts of the country. Just a few miles west of Meadhope there were animals remaining in the fields, with farmers living in terror of what the next inspection of their stock might show. As a sharp reminder of what could happen, the inquest into Colin Bell's death took place, with the inevitable verdict of suicide. Rosalind, one of the principal witnesses, found it all a deeply painful experience, reviving her sense of inadequacy.

The usual summer fixtures of garden fêtes and craft shows had all been cancelled. Throughout the dale, farmers were still isolated on their farms, shut in with their fears. Around Meadhope, where the worst had already happened, some families began to move about again, to go to the pub, to take a shopping trip to one of the nearby towns, to come to church. In fact, Rosalind's regular congregation grew steadily; she began to visit some of the farmers in her parish again, though she always checked beforehand to make sure she would be welcome. Each time, she had to pray for courage before making such a visit, for she knew she would be used as a sounding board for all the anger and bitterness and despair of her parishioners. She would carry that misery home with her afterwards, take it into church with her and try to shed it during a time of quiet prayer. But it was hard, and several times she went instead to see her old friend and mentor, Richard Fryer. He had little sympathy with country people, looked at from the desperate poverty and hopelessness of his own blighted urban parish. In her early days at Meadhope they had thought more or less alike on the subject; now, Rosalind found she had moved on, come to know and understand much more of the difficulties her parishioners faced in their daily lives, and particularly in the horror of these days. So though she talked to Richard, and found some help simply in doing that, it was to her father she turned as she had never done before, with long calls several nights a week, and he became her chief confidant. She thought he was enjoying this vicarious experience of a country parish. He had already agreed, eagerly, to come to Meadhope in August to cover for Rosalind so that she and Alasdair could go away over her birthday. As for where they would go, that was to be a surprise. All she knew so far was that he planned to visit his mother in a few weeks' time.

Josh's term ended and he came home, penniless and without any immediate plans to look for paid vacation work. 'I'll find something,' he assured Rosalind, who was not looking forward to the prospect of weeks under the same roof as a restless young man without the means to amuse himself. Fortunately, Josh liked walking, but it was also obvious to Rosalind that he still had designs on Lisa Robson, and to get anywhere with her he would need money, if only to buy her the occasional drink. On the other hand, the demonstrations at the burial site were still going on, if with rather less support and enthusiasm than in the early days. Josh, without enough money even for his bus fare, but with impressive devotion – to the girl rather than the cause, Rosalind thought – was prepared to walk up to Black Fell and back if no lift from his parents was forthcoming.

After two weeks at home, he found temporary bar work in a local country hotel, for a few hours at weekends. He did not like losing his valuable social time to the work, but put up with it for the sake of the minimal earnings. So long as he was making enough to be able to take Lisa out for a drink after their sessions at the site, then that was enough. Rosalind was concerned about his obsession with the girl. 'He seems to think of nothing else,' she said to Alastair, just after their son had left the house one morning.

'Don't you remember what it was like at that age, to be in love?'

'I suppose so. But I can't help thinking that if he was going to get anywhere with her, he would have done so long ago. I have the distinct impression she thinks of him as just a friend.'

'Friends can turn into something more, you may recollect,' said Alastair gently. 'Sometimes it just takes a while.'

She grinned. 'Yes, I remember. Point taken.' She linked her arm through his. 'Funny, isn't it, how different things look from the perspective of a parent? We end up worrying about things we thought nothing of when they happened to us. Just think what our own poor parents had to go through!'

'My mother didn't know the half of it,' Alastair admitted. 'I reckoned that way she wouldn't worry. Though I suppose she did anyway. Just about the wrong things.'

'Whatever you worry about, there's not much you can do, is there? I suppose we just have to let Josh make his own mistakes. I only hope Lisa and Scott aren't together any more. I have the impression they're not, but if they are, then Josh really hasn't a hope.'

Rosalind would have been reassured to know that Lisa and Scott were no longer an item, in any real sense. This time it was Scott's doing. He told himself that Lisa was a typical student – and a townie at that – with scant knowledge of what country life was really like. They had nothing in common, and a relationship between them was a hopeless prospect. Since one look at her was liable to send all his resolution toppling, he avoided her as far as possible, concentrating instead on his work, trying not to think of the other thing that hung over him, shadowing his life – the continuing rift with his father.

As far as his father was concerned he really had tried this time. He had worked hard at the project he wanted to put before him, working out all the details fully before speaking about it to his mother. She had been enthusiastic and had felt, as he did, that this might provide the opportunity they both wanted. He'd tried to speak to his father on the phone, but Dave still slammed down the receiver at the sound of his voice. Linda, too, tried several times to speak to him about Scott's proposals, but the result was always the same – he had no son, he wanted to hear no more about it. Linda continued to meet Scott with reasonable regularity, but was still the only member of his family he ever spoke to, though occasionally he would glimpse one of his sisters on their way to or from school. If they saw him, they gave no sign of it.

At the end of July it was Scott's birthday. His mother treated him to lunch, but there was nothing else to mark the day; nothing from his sisters, nor from his father. What was more, his mother had to report that yet another attempt to talk his father round had failed.

'Do you think he'll ever come round?' Scott asked bleakly.

'I don't know, pet. I just don't know.'

Meanwhile, time was passing. Before long the peak gardening season would be over and his source of income would disappear, or be reduced to occasional hedge cutting or mowing. As it was, he still wasn't earning enough to pay Elaine Robson an economic rent. Returning to Rose Cottage after work on his birthday, he stood in front of the mirror in the chintzy bedroom and took a long, hard look at his reflection. He was nineteen today, a slim dark lad, nice enough looking, but without a home of his own, shut out by his family, and without anything anyone would recognize as a proper job. He no longer even had a girlfriend to keep him here. So why was he staying in Meadhope? On the off chance that his father would come round? Even his mother seemed to have lost hope of that.

He drew himself up, squared his shoulders, took a deep breath. 'Right, Scott my lad,' he told himself. 'One last fling, then tomorrow you start looking for real work. Somewhere you know you'll find it. Time to get a life.' He wished that making the decision made him feel better about things. Instead, he simply felt he wanted to get very drunk.

So that was precisely what he did, calling up two of his friends to meet him in the Drovers, where they quickly got very drunk indeed. It was when they'd got to the rowdy singing stage and were about to be ejected by the landlord that Scott suddenly grew sick of the whole thing, said goodnight to his friends and staggered off towards home – or what passed for home. On the way, he found himself alongside the Royal Oak – quiet, respectable – and saw Lisa

150

sitting all alone at a table near the window. Lurching through the doorway, he made his way towards her.

'Hi!' He was swaying a little as he spoke, so sat rather suddenly down on the stool facing her.

'Hi!' There was something odd about her expression, though he wasn't sure what it was. 'I'm not stopping long,' she added.

'It's my birthday,' he told her. For the first time today, it really felt like it. To find Lisa just sitting here waiting for him was precisely what he needed to transform a bad day.

'I know. I gave you a card, remember?'

He supposed he remembered. 'You're all alone.'

'Not really,' she said. He followed her glance towards the gents, from which Josh Maclaren was just emerging.

Scott felt a surge of rage. So the day hadn't suddenly got better after all; it was ending exactly as it had begun – badly. He lumbered to his feet just as Josh reached them. 'What are you doing here?' he demanded.

'Having a quiet drink with my friend Lisa,' said Josh. He was by no means drunk, though he'd had enough to increase his self-confidence. 'I suggest you leave us alone.'

Scott tried, not quite successfully, to focus his gaze on the freckled face of his rival. 'Oh, you suggest I . . . that . . . do you? Well, you know what you can do with your suggestion!' He gave Josh a shove; ineffectual enough, but it enraged Josh into shoving him back.

'Go away! Get out of here!'

'Josh, don't!' Lisa intervened. 'It's—'

But Josh wasn't listening. As Scott shoved him a second time, sending him stumbling back against the adjacent table, he lost his temper completely and hit out with his fist. Scott staggered, swayed, then finally lost his balance and crashed to the floor, hitting his head on a stool on his way down.

'Look what you've done!' cried Lisa, flinging herself on the floor beside a dazed-looking Scott. There was blood pouring from a cut in his cheek.

Two large men, the landlord and a friend, appeared suddenly beside them. 'You two – out!' One of them took hold of Josh's collar, the other helped Scott to his feet. Then they marched them to the door and flung them out on to the street.

Lisa followed in dismay. 'Don't! He's hurt! Can't you see?'

Scott was on the ground again, though they'd been less rough with him than it appeared; he was simply unable to stand any more. He sat hunched in a heap on the pavement with his hand to his head, moaning. Lisa crouched down beside him, examining the profusely bleeding cut. 'We'll have to get him to hospital,' she said without looking up.

Josh, who had been hovering, appalled, ashamed, beside her, said, 'I'll get the car,' and turned and ran up the lane towards the rectory, where he burst, gasping, into the sitting room. 'Mum, Dad, we need help!'

Without pausing to ask any questions, Rosalind got the car out and drove round to Front Street, and then helped Scott gently into the vehicle. Josh and Lisa both insisted on coming too. Rosalind drove them to the hospital, where five stitches were put in Scott's cheek. Lisa stayed with him while this was done, leaving Josh and Rosalind to sit alone in the A&E waiting area. 'Now,' said Rosalind, 'perhaps you'd better tell me exactly what happened.'

Josh tried to do so, but he found it difficult to recall exactly how an undignified shoving match had so quickly turned into something much more serious. 'I never meant it to happen,' he said. 'Do you think I'll get taken to court?'

'I suppose that'll depend on how Scott feels about it,' Rosalind said. 'Or even the landlord.' She would have scolded Josh much more than she did, but she could see how miserable he was about the whole thing. Apart from anything else, it rather looked as if he'd now lost any chance he might have had with Lisa.

Much later, as she drove the silent trio back to Meadhope, an idea began to take shape in Rosalind's head. Could this unpleasant event – which might yet have serious consequences for her son – be offering just the opening she and Scott were looking for? Outside Rose Cottage, as she helped Scott – rather more sober now – out of the car, with Lisa his tender support on the other side, she asked, 'Would you like me to phone your parents and let them know what's happened?'

'Dad won't care,' said Scott. 'But OK, you could let Mam know.'

Which gave her the authority to telephone Middle Byers. She went to the study as soon as she got home and dialled the number, all the while praying that this call might be used to the good. It was Scott's father who answered. 'Dave, I'm very sorry. I know it's late. I – I hardly know how to put this. It really shouldn't have happened, and for my own son to be responsible . . .'

'What is this?'

'It's Scott—' She heard the exclamation at the other end of the line, and sensed that Dave was about to slam down the phone. 'No, wait a minute. He's hurt. Scott's hurt.'

'Hurt? Badly hurt? What happened?'

'There was a fight – well, a row anyway. Between him and Josh. Over a girl. He's had to have stitches and he's pretty shaken up.' She wondered if she'd made it sound more alarming than it was, but decided not to correct any false impression. Better that Dave should be more concerned than he need be, in the circumstances.

She heard a murmured conversation, and guessed that Linda had come to see what the call was about. The next moment, Linda herself was on the line, asking anxious questions. At the end, she said, 'I'll be down to see him as soon as I can. Thanks for letting us know.'

Rosalind prayed a little longer for the damaged family. Then she went in search of Josh. She found him sitting on a stool in the kitchen, staring gloomily into space. There was an empty mug in front of him, and the kettle had just boiled. Rosalind set to work to make him a coffee, then put her arm about him as she set it down.

He looked round. 'Don't start on at me, Mum. I know it was wrong. I never meant it to happen. I'm sorry.'

'Are you in a state now to tell me any more about it?'

So he did, as far as he could. It all seemed rather confused and pointless – as it had been, of course. 'The trouble is,' he ended, 'I just fancy her so much. I thought we were getting somewhere. She said she wasn't with Scott any more – I asked her, after what you said.'

'But?'

'Well, I think she'd like to be – with him, I mean. Oh, Mum, what am I going to do? Do you think they'll take it to court?'

'I rather doubt it, but we'll have to wait and see.'

At Rose Cottage, Lisa helped Scott to bed and then sat with him in case he should show signs of concussion, though the doctor had suggested that a severe hangover in the morning was the most likely result of the evening's events. For now, he seemed oddly content, just lying there holding her hand.

It was nearly midnight when the front doorbell rang. She hurried to open it before it wakened her mother, who would certainly be angry. There, as she had expected, stood Linda Emerson. 'He's in bed. He's OK,' Lisa said at once. 'Come on up.'

She led the way up the stairs and pushed open the door of Scott's room. Then she left them alone together. Some time later, Linda came in search of her, where she was drinking coffee in the kitchen. 'Want one?' asked Lisa.

Linda shook her head. 'I was going to take Scott home with me tonight, but since he's in bed, he's best staying here for now. So I'll fetch him after work tomorrow. He can come back for his bike some other time.'

It felt very strange driving into the farmyard, so familiar, so longed for, and now so spotlessly clean and empty, as he'd never seen it before. 'What will Dad say?' Scott had asked when, to his amazement, his mother had told him she was taking him home.

'I didn't leave him any choice,' Linda said. Though in reality they both knew that if Dave had forbidden her to bring Scott home, then she would have obeyed him, knowing that to be face to face with his father's anger in his present state would have been too much for her son to bear.

They could see Dave looking out of the window as they got out of the car, but when they went into the house he was nowhere to be seen. Scott could feel his heart pounding with anxiety. Would he find that anything had changed, or would his father continue to treat him as if he were not there; or worse, as if he were sheltering his bitterest enemy?

The two of them met over supper. Scott was already at the table, where he had been sitting while his mother made the last preparations for the meal. Jade had come in, grinned at her brother, come to hug him briefly, resting her head on his arm before going to take her own place. Then Vicky and Dave came in together. It was obvious to Scott that his sister was watching Dave, taking her cue from her father as to how she should treat her unexpectedly returned brother. Scott tried an uncertain smile. Dave said nothing, but nodded towards his son. It was hardly the warmest of welcomes, but it was a good deal better than Scott had feared; he still felt the thud of anxiety, but it had lessened now. Dave sat down at the opposite side of the table from his son. Vicky too gave a nod towards Scott, and then, her curiosity becoming too much for her, began to question him eagerly as to how he had come by his injuries. She was disappointed by his reply, because he simply said it was a stupid thing that wouldn't have happened if he hadn't drunk too much. 'And let that be a warning to you!' their mother put in at that point. 'Beware the demon drink!' Then they all began to eat, the women of the family continuing the conversation among themselves, leaving father and son to devour their food in silence, heads bent over their plates.

For the time being, Scott had to be content with that one small sign that he was being tolerated, that he was not going to be turned out from his home again – or not yet at least. It was already better than he had feared. His sisters seemed to get used to him quickly, though he found Vicky had changed. She was now assertively part of the family; she had developed a strong relationship with her father, inclined even to boss him around in a way he would not have accepted from anyone else. She no longer seemed obsessed with boys and make-up and chatting for hours on her mobile phone. She still did those things, but she also helped with domestic tasks, and had even, astonishingly, taken over the farm accounts, transferred them to the computer and spent a good deal of time working on them. She even made suggestions that her father took seriously. In a way, the new Vicky made Scott feel more estranged than ever; he had not seen her change, though his mother had told him about it, and somehow her centrality to the household seemed to exclude him. It was quite clear that he was no longer the heroic older brother, to whom she looked up. She might forgive him for what had happened, but she still felt that there had been something requiring forgiveness.

As for Dave, he might have ceased to turn on his son with anger and bitterness, but he continued to avoid him. He spoke to him only when absolutely necessary, and never with real warmth. Scott tried not to let it worry him, told himself that at least things were better, that Dave would come round given time. Within three days he was feeling well enough to go back to his work in the churchyard and afterwards, to collect his bike from Rose Cottage, where he spent some time with Lisa. She made it clear that she was his, if he wanted. The trouble was that he was not sure now that he did want her. They had so little in common. Her whole way of looking at things was so typical of an incomer, full of fine-sounding talk about the environment, without any real understanding of life in the countryside. Yet he fancied her with an intense desire. Was it possible for them to have a relationship without quarrelling all the time?

The questions circled endlessly in his head as he rode home, finding no firm answer, no solution. Still worrying over them as he reached the farmyard, he dismounted and wheeled the bike into the furthest byre. He was just fastening the padlock on the door, when a voice behind him made him jump. 'What's this idea you have then?'

He swung round. Dave stood in the kitchen doorway,

watching him with an opaque expression. Scott coloured – was this an accusation? 'Idea?' he faltered.

'Your mam said you'd come up with some idea for the farm.'

'Oh, that!' He realized he was shaking. 'It was just . . . well, Mam said something once about how some farmers would be going over to arable after this. I thought – I'm good with machines. Small farmers can't afford big machinery. They have to hire in stuff. Well, we could buy one or two big items – we've got room to store them. I'd maintain them. We could hire them out, take on contract work. *I* could, I mean. Spare time, of course. I'd be working here the rest of the time.'

Dave's face still gave nothing away, though he had clearly been listening attentively. After a moment, he said, 'Could work. You come up with some figures and we'll take a look at it.'

'I've done some already.'

'Good. Then you'd best bring them to the office.' He turned and went back into the house. Scott paused just long enough to punch the air with delight, and then followed him. When he reached the office with a file clutched under his arm, he found not only his father and mother sitting there, waiting to hear what he had to say, but Vicky as well, perched on the revolving chair beside the computer, watching him with an alert, suspicious gaze.

It was then he realized just how much things had changed while he'd been away, how his sulky teenage sister had somehow turned into a valued part of the family. He saw, too, that – though she tried to hide it – she resented his return home, fearing that her new ascendancy was about to be threatened. Scott was glad to be home, glad that his father was now ready to talk to him – and to listen – but he recognized uneasily that life at Middle Byers was never going to be the same again.

Fifteen

Rosalind drove Alastair to the station at Durham and kissed him goodbye as the Edinburgh train screeched and rattled its way on to the platform. 'Sure you'll be all right?' he asked for the twentieth time.

'Of course! You know things are quieter now. I'll be fine.'

'Don't overdo it – promise?' Then he grinned ruefully. 'I don't know why I bother to say that. I know you won't take a scrap of notice.'

'Darling, you'll only be away for a week! I can't do much damage in that time.' She gave him a little shove. 'Hurry up now, or the train will go without you!'

It was as she drove home, alone, that it struck Rosalind how much she had depended on Alastair during the past months – far more than she had realized. Alastair was not a showy, exuberant, pushy sort of man, nor one who constantly wanted you to know that he was available if needed. He simply got on with being there, quietly carrying small burdens – domestic tasks, cooking meals, simply waiting quietly until she wanted to unload her thoughts and anxieties – and all those trivial, scarcely noticed things had made it possible for her to keep going when things got really difficult. Well, now she was going to have to manage on her own for a while; it was just as well the worst seemed to be over. She offered a little prayer of thanks for Alastair's steadfast support, along with a plea for his well-being during this time apart.

It was raining again, though not cold – typical summer weather. At the rectory, she ran the car into the garage and then dashed across the garden to the house, her coat over her head. Indoors, it was quiet and there was no sign of Josh – still in bed then, she assumed, it being only eleven thirty, rather early for a student with only minimal holiday employment, and nothing else to get up for. Since the incident with Scott he had become noticeably depressed. Rosalind knew guilt had something to do with it – after all, Josh had never in his life resorted to violence, and though this might be a very tepid example, it was still a serious aberration in his eyes. But worse for him, of course, must be his realization that Lisa was never going to care for him, so long as Scott was around. Rosalind suspected that, at best, he'd been someone to pass the time with while Scott was unavailable – perhaps even a means of rousing Scott's jealousy, in which case it had succeeded brilliantly. Rosalind did not know whether or not the two of them were officially together again, but guessed that it would make no difference to Josh. Even the fact that neither Scott nor the landlord of the Royal Oak was interested in pressing charges against him seemed to be of little consolation to someone who felt his life had fallen apart. He had even stopped going to the demonstrations at the burial site; without Lisa, he was no longer interested.

Rosalind made herself a mug of coffee and then sat down to concentrate on the final details of the agenda for tonight's PCC meeting. Nothing very difficult, she thought, though you could never tell. Sometimes the most innocuous-looking item – settling the date of a sale of work, for instance – could prove to conceal the most painful of snares and lead to endless argument and displays of temper. And as yet she did not know all the members well enough to anticipate who was likely to be provoked by which issue. At Coldwell she had eventually been able to plan the meetings in such a way as to minimize the possibility of unnecessary conflict; but it had taken years of practice, and even then you could never be sure.

From the further corners of the house she could now hear sounds of movement – a door banging shut, water running.

Josh was out of bed then. He would be thinking in terms of breakfast, just as she was ready for lunch. She went to the kitchen and took bacon, eggs, mushrooms and tomatoes from the fridge – more than her lazy son deserved perhaps, but they would both enjoy the rare treat, and it was an opportunity for some mother and son quality time. She got everything ready, bar the cooking, and then called upstairs. 'All day breakfast, Josh!'

There was an answering groan from upstairs, and when her son at last reached the kitchen she saw she had misjudged the situation – 'hangover' was written all over his pale, scowling face. 'Just coffee, Mum,' he managed, before sinking on to a stool with his hand to his head.

'Good night then?' she asked, though she knew it had probably been more a case of drowning his sorrows. She wished he could have found some other salve than this, but was wiser than to say so.

His only response to her question was 'Humph!'

She made him coffee and assembled a bacon sandwich for herself, at which point Josh thought he could manage something of the kind too. By the time he'd finished eating it, he was sufficiently recovered to say, 'Next time I'm about to go out on the piss, tell me I'm grounded.'

'And how do I know you're going on the piss then?' she asked ruefully. 'Is that every time you go out after dark?' At the moment that was probably true, she thought.

'Not any more,' he said. 'I'm staying in tonight. Promise. If I look like going out, stop me.'

'It'll be a pleasure,' she said. 'Now, if you want to make yourself useful this afternoon, I've got Sally Oldfield coming to work on the parish web site.'

'I could have done that!'

'I know you could, but I thought it would help Sally.' As it might have helped Josh, she thought guiltily. It was the old story – how far should she put her parishioners before her family? And would doing so mean that she was neglecting her family, that they would suffer because of it? 'Anyway, you can still help me with this,' she went on quickly. 'I'm long overdue for a visit to the Old Rectory nursing home, so I'd be grateful if you could make sure Sally has all the coffee and biscuits she wants, and anything else she needs. OK?'

She waited until Sally had arrived – she was very obviously nearing the end of her pregnancy, but looked glowingly happy, not at all like someone who needed distraction – and was comfortably settled before the computer in the study, and then she walked round to the nursing home in the beautiful old stone building that had once been the rectory. A new annexe, discreetly built on behind the mansion, housed the unit for patients with dementia, so she went there first, to take a brief service which she hoped would bring some comfort to them. Then she made individual visits to the more clear-headed residents in the other part of the home. By the time she left, it was only five minutes to evensong, so she went straight to church, where she offered prayers for her son, as well as for the old people she had met today.

Back at the rectory, she went at once to the study. There was no sign of Sally, but Josh was seated in front of the computer – though to her surprise he was reading. He started as she came in, then shoved the book hurriedly back into the shelf beside him. He looked so embarrassed that Rosalind refrained from asking him what it was. In any case, he began hastily to explain that Sally had left, but the web site was much improved, something he demonstrated to his mother. Later, when he'd gone to choose a video at the newsagents, Rosalind looked to see which book he had been so furtively reading. The volumes near her desk were all devotional works, from many sources. She wasn't sure, but she thought it might have been St Augustine's *Confessions*, though that seemed an unlikely choice. On the other hand, she thought with amusement, St Augustine turned to God only after a misspent youth – maybe there was a fellow-feeling there.

Swallowing a hastily prepared meal, Rosalind set out for the PCC meeting, leaving Josh to amuse himself with a video and an early night. Fortunately, there were no hidden snares in tonight's meeting, and it was over in less than two hours. Josh had gone to bed by the time she reached the house, but there were two messages left in his angular scrawl on a scrap of paper on the hall table. 'Dad rang – arrived safely. Sends love. Uncle Jack rang. Please phone back tonight, however late.' Jack was the eldest of her brothers; the message sounded urgent. She glanced at the clock. It was nearly ten, a bit late for some people, and Josh might have misjudged the situation and overemphasized the urgency. Well, she'd have to take the chance. She dialled the number and waited.

Jack's voice was neutral but grave until, hearing who was speaking, it filled with relief. 'Rosie! Thank God! When you weren't in . . . I didn't want to leave a message, not about this.' Rosalind's heart thudded. It *was* bad news then, the very worst. 'It's Father. He had a severe stroke this morning – they rushed him to hospital. Then he had another two. He died early this evening, without regaining consciousness.'

She felt suddenly bereft of breath, as if someone had struck her a blow in the stomach. Her father was dead. That warm, authoritative voice on the end of the phone, the note of pride when he spoke of her achievements, the lively interest in all she did, in how her experience differed from his and how it was the same; the love that was utterly dependable – they had all gone from her life, suddenly, without allowing any time to prepare for their absence. She felt tears spring to her eyes.

'Rosie?' Jack sounded anxious, alarmed by her silence.

'Yes – it's OK. It's just . . . such a shock. He hadn't been ill, had he?'

'Not that we knew. He'd not been near a doctor for months. Which means there'll have to be a post-mortem, of course, unfortunately.'

'How's Mother?'

'Shocked, but busy doing lots of practical things. You know how she is. I don't think it's even begun to sink in.'

'Can she cope with putting me up? I'll have to rearrange things here, but I'll be down as soon as I can.'

162

'I'm sure it'll help to have you there. I imagine she'll want you to conduct the funeral. Could you do that?'

'I don't know, I really don't. Let's see what happens shall we? How are you and the others?'

'Oh, you know. He was an old man, of course. But we still didn't expect . . . well, not like this. The only thing is, he didn't hang on, sick and dependent. It's better for him that way. Anyway, let me know when you're coming, if you want meeting from any trains or whatever.'

Rosalind put down the receiver and then sat for a long time by her desk, staring into space. It was too late to make any arrangements for her absence tonight. She would have to contact the area dean to arrange cover for Sunday's services, and inform the churchwardens and PCC secretary; then there were her shifts on the helpline to rearrange. She would have to make those calls in the morning. Even Alastair . . . no, she couldn't disturb him now, because in doing so she would disturb his mother, who had a phone beside her bed and was a light sleeper. But she did get up early, about six thirty every morning. Rosalind could phone soon afterwards.

Meanwhile, there was the night to get through. She slept very little, and spent much of the time with the light on, though she could neither read nor pray. She simply lay there with nothing in her mind that could be called thought, but was more like a succession of disconnected memories – or rather not disconnected, for the common thread was her father, in particular the words he had spoken during their last telephone conversation, following the inquest into Colin Bell's death. 'Leave it all to God's mercy and compassion. In the end that's all you can do. It'll be enough; it's always enough.'

She dozed a little just as it was getting light, but was still out of bed by six. She longed for Alastair, for his voice, his arms about her. She was not hungry, but managed coffee and a slice of toast, more to fill the time than anything else. As soon as it got to seven o'clock she dialled Jessie Maclaren's number. 'I'm sorry to phone so early—' She braced herself for the inevitable reaction.

163

'Oh, this isn't early! I've been out of bed for a good while now. One doesn't wish to waste—'

Rosalind could have recited the words from memory, but instead broke in, 'Jessie, do you think I could speak to Alastair? It's urgent, I'm afraid.'

'I shall wake him.' And would enjoy doing it, Rosalind knew. Jessie had a self-righteous disapproval of those who willingly lay in bed later than she did, which was most of the world.

A little later, Alastair's voice, husky with sleep, came on the line. Oh, how she wished he were here! She told him quickly what had happened.

'Oh my darling, just when I'm not there! I'm so sorry! I'll come back at once, of course.'

Rosalind fought an impulse to urge him to do exactly that. 'No, wait a while, until I've got things sorted out here – and until I've a better idea of how soon the funeral's to be and everything. I'd like you to be there for that, of course. I just wanted you to know what had happened. I'll get in touch again later today. If you go out, keep your mobile switched on.'

It took her most of the morning to make all the necessary arrangements, and also to make a long call to her mother, who sounded calm – unnaturally calm, Rosalind thought – but was clearly pleased that she was intending to come to stay as soon as possible. Josh, wakened mid-morning, was told the news, which he took with a proper display of concern but no very deep feelings. His grandfather lived too far away, and visits between them were too infrequent for them ever to have become very close. He offered to come with Rosalind but she felt that, for now, it would be better for her to be alone with her mother, so they agreed he should stay at the rectory until his father returned. They would come to the funeral together. Sophie, phoned too in the course of that morning, also agreed to come for the funeral, as soon as its date was known.

Rosalind would have driven to her mother's, but knew that after her sleepless night and in her present emotional state that was hardly wise, so she booked a taxi to take her to the station. Jack met her at the other end and drove her to her parents' house – her *mother's* house, where Anne Percival welcomed her with a long, silent hug.

It made things more bearable for Rosalind to be near her mother, to help her with planning the funeral – though to her relief it was to be conducted by the parish priest, who had long been a family friend. Then there were the letters that came every day, as a result of the notice in the *Church Times*, from all over the country, from all the parishes in which William Percival had served, from people he had known at various stages of his life, both friends and parishioners and others he had met only briefly, who yet wrote of how deeply he had touched their lives. The letters often brought tears to Rosalind's eyes, and to her mother's, but they brought comfort too. 'He was a good man,' Anne said simply, as she finished reading the day's quota of letters on the eve of the funeral.

The church was thronged the next day. Josh came with Alastair, and Sophie arrived separately, at the last moment. She was not alone; with her was a tall, open-faced young man with fair curly hair, rather older than she was, and suitably dressed in dark suit and tie. 'This is Danny,' said Sophie, her casual tone belied by the fierce red that spread over her face.

There was no time for further introductions or explanations, so Danny joined the family group walking behind the coffin into the church. William Percival would have savoured the unexpectedness of it, Rosalind thought. Glancing at her mother, walking ahead with her arm linked through her eldest son's, she caught a tremulous smile, full of amusement. 'Trust Sophie,' Anne murmured. 'Your father will be chuckling over it.' Then she added, 'Life goes on.' It was said not with resentment or bitterness, but with optimism.

Sixteen

The promised holiday for Rosalind's birthday did not happen. She had already been absent from the parish for nearly two weeks following her father's death, and in any case William Percival was no longer available to provide cover for her, nor could anyone else be found at such short notice during the school holidays. 'We'll go away later, maybe after Harvest Festival,' Rosalind promised an exasperated Alastair when they had been home for a week after the funeral. It was a Saturday morning and they were sitting over coffee in the kitchen; later that day Rosalind had the postponed wedding to conduct for the Hall family, a rather more subdued affair than had originally been planned. Rosalind had prepared the talk she would give with great care. Now, she was allowing herself a little time with Alastair.

'And when's that, pray?'

'September some time. The sixteenth, I think. I'm going to have to think it out very carefully this year.'

'When do you ever do anything else?' Alastair demanded, in a tone that mingled respect and impatience. In past years at Coldwell, she had used the harvest festival as a time to remind her parishioners of the needs of their fellow human beings in other places, who faced real hunger and greater hardship, because of drought or war. Alastair had to acknowledge that it would be difficult to persuade the farmers of Meadhope, in their bitterness and anger, that there were others suffering more than they did – but then, perhaps Rosalind wouldn't try. 'Maybe by then foot-and-mouth will be so far behind us, everyone will be able to feel thankful.'

166

'Oh, I do hope so! It certainly seems to be on the way out. Though Linda Emerson believes that's because they've stopped reporting it, and that it hasn't gone away at all. I hope she's wrong. The trouble is that everyone's so paranoid that they go on believing the worst, no matter what. I suppose that's understandable.'

'Let's hope they have a full-scale inquiry and learn some lessons from it all.'

'I gather that's what they said last time, yet no one learned anything as far as anyone can see. It's no wonder farmers think no one understands them or speaks for them.'

Alastair grinned. 'You'll be joining the Countryside Alliance next!'

'Not me. Not so long as they talk about hunting being a "human right". That's grotesque. That sort of talk's enough to turn me into a rabid anti-hunt fanatic, which I never have been. But the other things they . . .'

They heard the front door open and close. Josh had gone out soon after breakfast, telling them only that he was going for a walk. It was part of an odd pattern that his life seemed to have taken on since coming home from the funeral. He had begun to get up early, never went out at night, and spent much of each day either shut in his room or going for long walks – on the main roads of course, as the footpaths were still closed. He did not seem unhappy exactly, just subdued and pensive, but the change was sufficiently marked for his parents to have given it some anxious discussion. Rosalind called to him. 'There's some coffee, Josh!' He came in and poured himself a mug. 'Good walk?' Rosalind asked. Had he perhaps gone out hoping to bump into Lisa, by chance, as she and Alastair had thought he might be doing? If so, there was nothing in his expression that indicated either elation or disappointment. 'Are you working tonight?'

'Yes.' He took a gulp of coffee. 'Mum and Dad – I've been thinking. About next year, when I get my degree.'

'And go on to get some massively well paid job in the city,' commented Alastair, echoing what Josh had always claimed he wanted to do. 'Yes?'

'I think I might put in for VSO – you know, Voluntary Service Overseas. Just for a year, see how it goes.'

They gazed at him in astonishment. First the demonstrations at the burial site, now this! Had his pursuit of Lisa accidentally led him to develop a social conscience? 'What brought this on?' Rosalind asked.

He shrugged. 'Don't know really. I just didn't seem to be doing much with my life. Sort of drifting. Thought I should try something worthwhile for a change.'

'Good for you!' Rosalind exchanged a glance with Alastair, who clearly shared her wonderment – and pleasure too.

Josh took another gulp of coffee and then sat for a time gazing into his mug. Then, as if suddenly deciding to be more open about his feelings, he went on, 'There were all those letters people sent when Grandad died. All those people who said their lives had changed because of him. I thought, no one's ever going to say that about me, not the way I'm going. So I've decided to do something about it.'

'I can tell you one person whose life's changed because of you,' said Rosalind wryly. 'Scott Emerson.'

'That's just what I mean. The only thing I've got to my name is injuring some guy I don't know over a girl who's not interested in me.'

'That wasn't what I meant. It may not be what you intended to happen, but if it wasn't for you Scott might not be back home again, helping his father revive the farm. And I've seen him and Lisa going about together again too, which I know isn't at all what you wanted, but is probably for the best.'

'Well, maybe. But I was lucky, wasn't I? It might have gone badly wrong for everyone. I'd rather get my life on track so that good things happen *because* of what I'm doing, not in spite of them.'

Alastair laid a hand on his shoulder. 'Good for you, lad! We're proud of you.'

Josh grinned. 'Thanks for being the sort of parents who don't mind if I don't make pots of money.'

'Oh, you're not let off the hook altogether,' Alastair joked. 'By the time we retire, we shall expect you to be able to keep us in the manner to which we wish to become accustomed.'

'Don't look at me! There's always Sophie, remember.' Sophie was now working with her chosen practice in the Lakes and sharing a house with Danny, the young man who had come with her to the funeral. He was Irish, a vet well established in an adjoining practice of which he was a full partner, being eight years older than Sophie. Before long, Sophie's parents hoped to get to know him better than the brief meeting at the funeral had allowed. 'He seems nice,' was the only verdict they had been able to come up with so far.

'Hmm,' said Alastair. 'A vet – not a bad salary. But we had rather hoped for better.'

Josh grinned, and then began to show them the various pieces of information about VSO he'd downloaded from the Internet.

When the time came, Alastair and Rosalind did mark Rosalind's birthday, but with a simple day trip to the coast, followed by dinner in a favourite restaurant. It was while driving home afterwards that Alastair turned on the radio for the news headlines, and they heard that there was a suspected case of foot-and-mouth disease in south-west Northumberland, just over the border from the dale.

'Oh dear Lord, no!' murmured Rosalind.

'The tests might prove negative. There've been a few scares lately that haven't led to anything.'

But none so near as this, thought Rosalind.

The tests were positive, and a cluster of other cases followed. New notices appeared, dividing the countryside into blue and red boxes, according to the closeness of the danger; red areas were virtual no-go areas. On all the roads through and around the dale barriers were set up, and each vehicle that passed was sprayed with a fierce jet of disinfectant. Rosalind felt as though everyone was holding their breath in terror of the worst. For the scattering of farmers who had begun, tentatively, to restock, it was a dreadful time. They knew there were some in this new outbreak who had now been hit twice. How could anyone survive such a blow? The clergy met to discuss reopening the helpline, which had been closed down due to lack of interest about a month ago. In the end, they decided to wait and see what happened. By now, there were many more helplines and other points of contact than there had been at the outset. Daphne Wynyard, like many others, was fully involved again with the Countryside Alliance and its plans to put massive pressure on the government. 'I know you think we're just the hunting, shooting, fishing crowd,' Daphne reproved Rosalind one day. 'But we aim to speak for every true countryman and woman, for all their interests.'

'But don't those interests sometimes clash? And isn't it going to muddle things if you try and represent every-body?'

'Not if we say what we really want loudly enough – which is for a government that actually cares for countryfolk and tries to meet our needs. We want a voice; we shall have one. We'll make the government listen, you mark my words!'

The following Monday was, as usual, Rosalind's day off. Having allowed herself a lie-in and a leisurely breakfast, she had then gone into the study to read mattins before setting out for a day shopping in Darlington. She was just stepping out of the door when she heard the phone ring. Regretting that she had delayed so long, she still had to resist an impulse to pick up the receiver. But she did listen carefully until the answerphone clicked in, just to hear who it was in case it was something she ought to deal with.

A woman's voice came on the line, urgent, sombre. 'Rosalind – it's Linda. Linda Emerson.'

Rosalind's heart thudded. How could she ignore this call? She lifted the receiver. 'Linda, Rosalind here, what is it?' Please let it not be some other dreadful blow for the family at Middle Byers, just when there seemed to be a glimmer of hope coming into their lives again! She had not heard that they'd restocked yet, but perhaps they had, just in these last few days, and then the disease had struck again.

'It's Sally Oldfield. Ben asked me to tell you. She's been rushed into hospital. The ambulance has just left. Ben went with her.'

Was this good news or bad? Surely it wasn't usual to send for an ambulance for a woman in labour, not if things were going normally and the family had a car. But perhaps it was different here in the country. 'Is it the baby? I can't remember when it's due. About now, isn't it?'

'Not for a few weeks yet. But something's gone wrong – I don't know what exactly, but they had to call the doctor in the middle of the night.'

Rosalind noted down the details, as far as Linda knew them, all the while sending up an urgent prayer. *Dear God, don't let them lose the baby, after all they've been through!*

At the end of the call, she glanced at the clock. The ambulance had left about an hour ago, so should have reached the hospital in Durham by now. Should she go there at once? That Ben had asked Linda to let her know what had happened suggested that he wanted her to be there. In any case, there were two patients in the hospital whom she had been intending to visit tomorrow; she could see them today, if she found that the Oldfields had no need of her.

She drove to the hospital and asked the way to the maternity unit, where she was told that Sally was in theatre, her husband with her. By the time she had made her two other visits, it was over. 'Mrs Oldfield's out of theatre. She's resting. If you wait here, I'll have a word with her husband.'

Nothing to tell her what had happened! Her inside twisting with anxiety, Rosalind waited for what seemed like hours, but was only a few minutes, before Ben himself appeared. He looked utterly exhausted, but calm. He even smiled.

'Thanks for coming. They weren't happy about the baby's

heartbeat. They had to do an emergency Caesarean. But everything's fine now. We've got a little girl.'

Relief flooded her. 'And she's all right?'

'Small, but perfectly formed. Come and look.' He led her to the window that looked on to the nursery, where his tiny daughter lay swaddled in a white hospital blanket in her crib. It was impossible to see what she looked like. 'We're calling her Grace.'

'That's pretty,' said Rosalind. And appropriate, she thought, wondering if they too looked on her as an out-pouring of God's grace. 'And how's Sally?'

'Very tired, but otherwise OK. They did the operation under epidural, so she knew what was happening. It was amazing, in spite of everything. I'll go and see whether she'd like to see you.'

The young mother smiled when Rosalind appeared at her bedside, and took her hand. 'Send up a thank you for us,' she asked softly.

Rosalind promised, offering a silent prayer at that very moment, both in thankfulness, and for the wellbeing of mother and baby in the days and weeks to come.

Seventeen

In those fearful early September days, the disease hovering so close to the borders of the dale steadied and then faded. There were no new cases after the first cluster, and none in the dale itself. In the country as a whole it seemed too as if the end was at last in sight. But Rosalind knew that the end of the epidemic would not mean the end of the suffering it had brought. It would be a very long time before the wounds truly healed, even once there were animals back in the fields, and everything had returned to what looked like normal. It would be like her pain at the loss of her father, a grief that would fade with time, but yet would always be there, because of what she had lost. Yet at least in losing her father she could find infinite cause for thankfulness – for what he had given her for so many years, for a life well lived. There was no such consolation for farmers who had lost their life's work.

And now it was nearly time for her first harvest festival at Meadhope. She had imagined it before she came here as something infinitely more meaningful than those at Coldwell, where many of those who came to worship probably had no idea where their food came from, or what harvest meant. Here in the country the very people who grew corn and raised animals would be giving thanks in person for the year's harvest. Yet now that it was upon her, she was faced with so many questions. What is there to be thankful for? What harvest is there for this beautiful, blighted dale? The burial site at Black Fell, the empty fields? The few fields of corn salvaged after a wet summer by farmers for whom it is all they have left of a once prosperous mixed farm? How could she ask those still living through the horror of it to be thankful for this year?

The date had been fixed for some time: Sunday September 16th. It had been printed in the magazine, and she had made sure that the ladies who organized the flowers had noted it in their diaries. She had also asked the Sunday school teachers to come up with ideas for involving the children, something they had discussed together just last week.

But that still left her part – to find the right theme for the day – and she was continuing to worry over it with only a few days to go. On the Monday beforehand she had her usual day off, and was at least able to find somewhere to walk, to think – not yet one of the now overgrown footpaths, but a quiet back road leading to nowhere in particular. She came home with her mind still full of confusion to find a message from John Parker on the answerphone. Since it sounded urgent, she phoned him back at once. 'They're closing the steelworks,' the minister said baldly. The small steelworks on the eastern edge of Meadhope was the chief employer in the town.

'But I thought it was doing well, order books full and all that?'

'Bad management, so I gather,' he said. She could hear the bitterness in his voice. 'As if there wasn't enough already.'

Even here! she thought, her memory going back to her first year at Coldwell, when the closure of a local factory had added another blow to an already blighted community. This would do the same, for farming could never meet all the employment needs of the dale – in fact many farming families, like the Emersons, depended on jobs outside the farm for their very survival. Daphne's right, she found herself thinking; the real danger facing the countryside is that it will become simply a pretty environment to live in – except that without the small farmers it won't remain pretty, but will simply revert to scrub and waste. She felt angry, looking for some answer. 'I suppose it's a bit early – or have any meetings been arranged?'

'You bet!' John said. 'Thursday night, village hall. We

hope to get one of the directors along. Ted Desmond's promised to be there, too.'

Rosalind was shuffling through her diary. 'Count me in as well,' she said. So here was one more thing that made thankfulness hard.

The following morning, having no other immediate calls on her time, she sat down to give her full attention to her harvest sermon, to try at least to settle on a theme that hit the right balance. By lunchtime she thought she had found it. She would speak of how we must all cling on to what is good in the hardest of times; to enjoy the moments of happiness, however fleeting; to savour every moment of peace and beauty; to be thankful for the way that so often, in adversity, friends and family give unstinting support. She still felt dissatisfied – it all sounded a bit trite, inadequate, and it somehow left out God. It was a message that could be offered to anyone, which was fine as far as it went. But was that what she wanted?

Deciding to leave it for the time being, she made a sandwich for her lunch and then set out on a round of visits to her housebound parishioners. First on her list was Alice Pearson, a frail widow in her nineties who lived in one of the terraced cottages near the steelworks, and passed her time crocheting blankets for Oxfam. 'I can't do much else now, can I?' she would say. 'But so long as I can do something, well then I'll keep at it.'

Rosalind banged the polished brass knocker but there was no reply. 'If you don't get an answer, just come on in – the back door's always open,' Alice often said. 'You know how I drop off. I don't always hear.' It worried Rosalind a little that she should be so trusting – no one in Coldwell would have risked leaving a door unlocked like that, but then Meadhope was not Coldwell. She did as she'd been told, and found Alice snoring gently in her armchair in her snug back parlour, while the television chattered away in the background. It showed two skyscraper blocks with planes crashing into them – some disaster movie, Rosalind thought, not Alice's sort of thing at all. She usually liked a good weepy romance, or an Agatha Christie. She must have been asleep for a good while.

'Alice!' Rosalind murmured.

With a final snort, Alice jolted awake, her blue eyes opening on Rosalind. 'Oh dear! Here I go again.' She got up unsteadily, moving to switch off the television – she had never got round to using a remote control. Then, halfway there, she stopped, staring at the screen. Rosalind looked again. It was there still, the picture of the two towers and the crashing planes, though now one of the towers was falling, then the other. She realized then, with horror, that it was no disaster movie; it was real, and it had just happened, was still happening, this very day.

Alice sat down again, and Rosalind took a seat beside her. The commentary on the television went over and over the story – the Twin Towers of the World Trade Centre in New York; the hundreds of people coming to work, starting a normal day; the two planes hijacked, looking so small, so innocent as they took their deadly course; the tiny figures leaping from one certain death to another as the towers dissolved into a mountain of dust and rubble. Against the commentary, Alice's voice, cracked with emotion, murmured, 'Terrible! All those poor people!' again and again. Eventually, as the tale was repeated over and over, Alice switched off the television. 'You'll say a prayer, Rosalind.'

So Rosalind prayed, for those who had died, and also for those who had perpetrated the horror, that any still living might have a change of heart, might learn to replace hatred and bitterness with love, and she prayed for an end to the evils that had caused such hatred and bitterness. Then, conscious that she would otherwise be leaving Alice alone with her thoughts, Rosalind stayed a little longer, talking of other, ordinary things: Alice's health, her family, the crochet work she had been doing.

By the time she left, it was too late for other visits. She went straight to the church for evensong, and found a congregation of three already there, waiting for her –

Keith Grey, Elaine Robson, and Josh, to her amazement. She said nothing, simply took her place and began to read the service, adding the special prayers that they must all feel were needed. Afterwards, Josh left quickly, with a casual wave in her direction, though the other two lingered for some time, talking of what had happened.

By the time she reached home, Josh was sitting in front of the television alongside Alastair, newly returned from work. Rosalind took pizzas from the freezer and they spent the evening together, just watching. At one point, Josh, beside her on the sofa, shifted closer to his mother, like a frightened child. Rosalind, glancing at Alastair at that moment, knew he had seen, and that he too was afraid. Suddenly the world seemed a terrifying place, where those who felt they had nothing to lose, who felt they had a just cause, could plan and carry out acts of unimaginable horror. And what would come from this? What might this mean for peace in the world? Would the world leaders – especially in America – show restraint and statesmanship? The signs were not good, but she could only pray.

The news was, of course, everywhere during the following days, occupying almost every page in the newspapers, filling hours of television. There were terrible pictures of rejoicing Palestinians; the more heartening messages of sympathy and support from the most unlikely sources; encouraging signs that the new president of the United States might show more restraint than so many had feared. Again and again, as she read and watched and listened, Rosalind wondered what her father would have made of it all, what he would have said. 'I keep wishing your father were here to talk it over with,' her mother said to her on the phone one evening, echoing her own feelings.

Then Thursday night came. It was as well Rosalind happened to look in her diary earlier in the day, or she would have forgotten completely about the meeting. As it was, she wondered as she set out if anyone else would turn up. The fate of one small steelworks must seem very insignificant set against the world-changing events of the past few days.

The hall was packed by the time Rosalind arrived, with men employed by the works, with their wives and families. It was a noisy, angry gathering, from which John Parker emerged to greet her. 'Ted Desmond's had to go back to London, but he's left a message of support for us to read out,' he said.

'Don't tell me – the managing director's suddenly got connections with New York and has chickened out.'

'No, he's here – or rather, one of his subordinates is. He's going to speak first. Will you join us on the platform?'

She did so, and heard the board's representative lavish praise on an excellent workforce – which brought shouts of derision from the floor – and then go on to promise that every effort would be made to find a buyer for the works. There was not much more to the meeting than that, but he could have been left in no doubt of the strength of feeling in the hall.

Afterwards, Rosalind lingered with the clergy and several of the employees at the works to discuss tactics. 'Foot-and-mouth's done its best to destroy this dale,' one man said. 'Farming laid waste, tourism on its knees. Well, they're not taking this from us as well.' As she walked home afterwards, Rosalind realized that no one had once mentioned the fall of the Twin Towers.

Talking to Alastair when she reached home, she commented, 'All the papers are saying things will never be the same again after this; the world has changed for ever, and all that stuff. But I'm not sure. It's terrible, of course it is, and on a scale never known before. But it's certainly not the first act of terrorism and it won't be the last.'

'It changes everything for the States, I fear,' Alastair said. 'They're just not used to terrorism on their own soil.'

'Perhaps. But even that's not the world. Yes, it makes everything seem much more uncertain and dangerous, but as much as anything that's because we're not sure we can trust Bush and his lot to behave wisely. But you talk to people here and it's just another bit of news. It certainly doesn't sweep everything else out of their heads.'

'We've got used to terrorism, I suppose.'

'More to the point, I think, their lives have already been turned upside down by foot-and-mouth. If you've just come through your own earthquake, you don't tend to look on other people's with anything more than a rather distant compassion. Life already looks very different for people here than it did a year ago. It's something like this threat to the steelworks that can push foot-and-mouth to the back of their minds for a bit, not something happening to other people on the other side of the world.'

'You have to admit though, there are things about this that are different from anything we've seen before – just the scale of it, for a start.'

'I know. And I tell you what else is new – the mobiles. It's what sticks in my mind most of all, those last calls to their loved ones. It's heartbreaking, yet . . . well, once, before mobiles, there would have been no last declaration of love, nothing, just an absence.'

The following morning, Rosalind drove up to Moor Farm to see the Oldfields about Grace's christening. The young couple now looked far removed from the exhausted pair she had seen in the hospital a few weeks ago, despite the inevitable broken nights of early infancy. Their happiness seemed to fill the house, shutting out all the horrors of the world beyond its walls. The baby too was clearly thriving, already several pounds heavier, her deep-blue infant eyes beginning to focus on objects and people about the room. She was, Ben told Rosalind with pride, an astonishingly peaceful baby, who fed and slept well, and was only seriously wakeful through the day. 'It's a funny thing,' he confessed, 'and I'm not saying I would ever have wanted foot-and-mouth to happen, or the killing of our animals. It was terrible, awful, and I still don't think it should have happened at all. It wasn't necessary. But it would have been much harder now if we'd had animals to see to as well as little Grace. A few hens are quite enough. It means we can both spend all the time we want looking after her.'

He glanced at Sally, and Rosalind saw the smile that flashed between them, tender and warm. 'Are you still thinking of selling up?'

'Maybe not.'

'Definitely not!' put in Sally. 'For one thing, cities don't seem such a safe bet after what happened on Tuesday. But we'll just have a few animals, more a hobby than a full-scale smallholding. I think it'll be good for Grace to grow up among animals – so long as all this doesn't happen again.'

'Well, if you're selling your meat, let me know. I'm going to be buying local produce as much as I possibly can.'

'Good for you! There'll not be much around yet, but when everyone gets back into full production, we're going to be needing all the help we can get. We're all going to have to diversify even more than we were before. I'm saying we, because we've got other plans ourselves, besides the animals. We're going to set up a support service for farmers and others in the dale – we've got plenty of computer expertise we can put to use, and there's a real demand.'

'Which means we'll be campaigning like mad for a broadband connection,' Ben said. 'It's crazy that areas like this should be without such a vital lifeline.'

'You can count me in on any new campaign,' promised Rosalind. 'That's one thing this year's taught me – even country parsons have to get up to date with the latest technology.'

'Well, we're here whenever you need technical support.'

They discussed the arrangements for the christening, which was to take place during the Sunday eucharist in a month's time, and then, after a cup of coffee and more admiration of the perfection that was little Grace, Rosalind drove home.

Suddenly the world seemed a more hopeful place. What was more, two words had stuck in her mind from her talk with Ben and Sally: lifeline, support. They seemed to fuse in her mind, sending out all kinds of connections. She knew she had her harvest sermon.

Eighteen

Rosalind made her way to church with her heart singing. Today, among the packed congregation in the church heavily fragrant with fruit and flowers, would be her daughter, and the young man she had brought with her to the funeral, Danny. They had turned up unexpectedly the day before, and it had been clear from the start that they were fizzing with excitement, though it was not until they'd all gathered in the sitting room before dinner that they made their announcement. 'Mum, Dad,' Sophie had said, in a tone that made both her parents sit absolutely still. 'Danny and I are getting engaged. We'd like to fix a date for our wedding, here at Meadhope, some time next year. Around Easter, say.'

It was hard after that to concentrate on the harvest service, to bring her thoughts into the right mood for the day. Rosalind knew that though *she* might feel full of joy and thankfulness, that was not how most of her congregation would be feeling. For them, there needed to be a graver, more profound message, given by someone who understood, as far as was possible, how they felt; someone who had come to see how she could 'speak to their condition'. There would also, after this last week, be those who came to remember the victims of the suicide pilots; she knew of one woman whose brother-in-law was thought to be among the dead, though his body would probably never be found. This was a solemn day, a time for recollection, with gratitude very far from the minds of most of those who came.

She walked across the tidy churchyard, trying not to think of Sophie's news, and the happiness it had brought, trying to bring herself to soberness. She recalled her first evening in this place, nearly eight months ago, how awed she had been at the prospect, yet how happy, looking forward to serving these people. She remembered the plans she'd made, the hopes she'd carried with her. Now, after a single summer, everything she had hoped for and planned and dreamed of was gone, wiped out. She had fumbled her way to a different course, through the chaos of this time, struggling to find where God was in it all. She had tried to the best of her ability to walk alongside her parishioners, to let God use her for their well-being. If in any way she had succeeded, then it was God's doing, not hers, for she had been quite unprepared for it, hampered by preconceptions, floundering in the debris left from the crashing of her dreams.

That first evening many of the same people had been present as were flocking here today – Elaine Robson, Sheila Morris, Linda Emerson, Keith Grey, Josh and Sophie. But this morning there were others, for all the Emersons were walking into the church with Linda, together, a united family; and Sally Oldfield was there too, having apparently left little Grace in the care of her father. And taking his place in the pew beside Sophie was Danny, now to be accepted as part of their own family; and the new, serious-minded, purposeful Josh, who would be returning to university next week.

Rosalind went to the vestry to robe for the service, before spending a little time in prayer for her own part in the worship, that it might be worthy and to the purpose. Then she prayed for the concerns that would be brought here today – the anger and bitterness and grief of the farmers; their sense that their whole way of life was threatened; the grief of those who'd lost loved ones in New York; the fear and insecurity that everyone must feel as a result of that atrocity.

Then, with a sudden shaft of insight, she saw a link between the suicide bombers, whose anger and alienation had made them use such desperate measures, and the blighted farming community. Of course, no farmer was going to stoop to such means, though Colin Bell's fate reminded her how real that desperation could be. But here in this land, farmers and country people felt alienated too, neglected and marginalized. But while none of them was going to turn to any solution so terrible, so drastic, if no one tried to listen they would certainly be driven to find more brutal ways of making their voices heard. Already Daphne Wynyard's beloved Countryside Alliance, while offering support and a voice to beleaguered country people, was threatening to become more extreme if they were not listened to. It was up to people like Rosalind, an incomer, a townie, whose own experience had brought her to a greater insight and understanding, and led her to question her old assumptions and preconceptions, to join her voice with theirs, so that it might be the more easily heard.

She prayed for them all, as in simpler terms she would do later, during the intercessions. Then she concentrated her mind on the central focus of the Eucharist, before going to take her place at the back of the church and give the signal to the organist – Alastair – to bring his solemn voluntary to an end and prepare for the first hymn. The packed congregation rose, the first glorious notes of the tune 'Blaenwern' soared into the vaulting, and the service began, not with 'We plough the fields and scatter', which would have been the traditional choice, but with the modern words of 'God is love; let heaven adore him', which spoke of God's triumphant love for his whole creation, his sharing in its grief and pain, but not at all of crops and harvest time.

The readings she had also chosen with care – passages that spoke of caring for the poor and the needy, rather than simply giving thanks for harvest time; and to the prayers she added the special collect for peace. Then she went to stand on the chancel steps for the sermon.

'We have come here today to offer our thanks to God,' she said. 'Yet I know that many of you are here for very different reasons. Perhaps we all feel at this time that there seems to be very little in our lives, or in the world around us, to be thankful for . . . Of course, it's right that we should pray for peace, for the needs of the world, for healing. But even for our own sakes, for our own well-being, we do also need to find a way to give thanks, because it helps us to see what is good both in our own lives and those around us . . . It is too easy, when things are going badly, to believe that what we are suffering is the whole story. When my father died, for a little while, nothing else mattered. I gave little thought to anyone else. But I was grateful for the support and love of friends and family, for those who tried to make things easier for me, here and at my parents' house. Above all, I was thankful for my father's long and good life.

'Even in our worst moments, there are always good things to be found. There is always hope. Above all there is always God's love, around and within us. Even in our darkest moments he is there with us, for every step of the way. Sometimes it's hard to feel his presence – very hard. But it's there, the lifeline to which we can cling when despair seems all around. Like the mobile phones at the Twin Towers, he is sending us his message of love – love complete and without conditions, love that is there to the very end, and beyond.

'Sometimes in our despair we think no one is listening. We think we are abandoned. Perhaps indeed we have been abandoned, in worldly terms . . . But if no one on earth is listening to us, if no human being is prepared to give us the least moment of attention and care, we are still never truly abandoned, for God is always there. He is always listening. He always cares. He always loves us. He may show that love through our family and friends and neighbours, for we are each one of us called to be his lifeline to those around us; but if we fail, if they fail us, *He* does not. He is there, not only listening, but acting, responding. He is the ultimate lifeline we can cling to in any of the difficulties and tragedies that life throws at us. He is the one lifeline that will never fail, the one true lifeline, for though he can make use of our gifts and strengths for his purposes, he does not rely on us for them – which is just as well.

'Yet we must all remember that we are called, not to happiness, riches, an easy life, but to service – service of God and our fellow human beings . . . If we put that first, if we set aside our own longings for peace and contentment, then we may find everything we could wish for, even in the midst of turmoil, through service to others, because we know that in serving others we are serving God himself. We are enabling God's power and love – God's lifeline – to reach out into the world. We can be the channels for his power and grace. That is an awesome responsibility, yet a heartening one, because we know that, however inadequate we are, with God's love we can do anything we are asked to do . . .'

After the service, as usual, Rosalind stood in the porch to greet the departing congregation. There were thanks from some, others talked of their own thoughts and difficulties. Daphne Wynyard was here this morning – Ashburn's harvest festival was the following week, but she explained that she had wanted to be at Meadhope today. As she gave Rosalind's hand a hearty shake, she said, 'I had my doubts when you arrived. Had you down as an ignorant townie. Maybe you were, then. But you've stood alongside us this ghastly year, you've shown you care, and understand too. I reckon you'll do.'

Rosalind was genuinely moved. There could be, she thought, no higher compliment. Later she walked home with Alastair for a celebratory lunch around the rectory table. The sun was shining at last and the first autumn colours were tinting the trees around the churchyard. Beyond, the green hills stretched against the sky. 'I love this place,' she said, as she slipped her hand into his.

'Then you don't wish you'd stayed in Coldwell, out of reach of foot-and-mouth? It's not exactly been your dream country parish, has it?'

'You can say that again! But all this . . . it's made me realize. Caring about the environment's all very well. But I think most green-minded liberals, like me and you, make one big mistake. We think of farmers and country people as a problem, an obstacle even, something standing in the way of a better environment. That's wrong. People who work on the land are as much a part of the environment as the trees and fields. In fact, they may be the most important part. After all, they've helped make it what it is. Those of us who want a better environment have to include the people who live in it in the picture, even put them first – especially here, where there are so many small farmers. Until we care for them, we can't begin to care for the things around them. After all, if they're forced off the land, for whatever reason, the balance of things will be upset for ever.'

Alastair slid an arm round her shoulder. 'I think you'd find Sophie agrees with you there,' he said.

Rosalind grinned. 'If she's capable of thinking of anything but Danny at the moment. What do you think of him?'

'Seems fine, so far. Nice sense of humour. So, how does it feel to be about to become a mother-in-law?'